Jerry Raine

was born in Yorkshire in Somalia and has also lived in Australia. Since leaving school he has worked in nineteen jobs, and can currently be found at London's Murder One bookshop. In 1986 he won the *Mail on Sunday* fiction prize. *Smalltime* is his first novel. He lives in Sevenoaks in southern England, where he plays guitar and writes songs.

Smalltime

Jerry Raine

BLOODLINES

First Published in Great Britain in 1996 by
The Do-Not Press
PO Box 4215
London SE23 2QD

A Paperback Original

ISBN 1 899344 13 6

British Library Cataloguing in Publication Data. A catalogue record for
this book is available from the British Library.

Printed and bound in Great Britain by The Guernsey Press Co Ltd.

For Rajini.

One

It was just a short walk to the nightsafe every evening, and Chris always went on his own.

Ron, the off-licence manager always said, 'If someone attacks you, just let them have the money.'

On this particular evening though, Chris was in a bad mood, and when the mugger came for him he reacted.

He was standing next to the nightsafe, by the side of Barclays Bank in a dark side street when, from the corner of his eye, he saw a figure approaching. Chris had the night-wallet in an orange carrier bag and he couldn't believe it when the man reached for it as he walked by.

Chris said, 'Shit,' and held on to the carrier as the man tugged and pulled him into the road, digging his feet into the tarmac, reacting before he had time to think. Then he was reaching for the man's throat, grabbing him by the collar of his leather jacket.

The man was breathing heavily as they tussled in the middle of the road. Luckily, no cars were coming. Chris tried to look up into the man's face, but all he could make out was his dark hair and a height of about six-one. The next thing he knew there was a fist coming towards him and his knees were giving way.

Chris hadn't been punched in the face for about fifteen years, and as he fell to the road he was seeing stars or maybe fireworks because it was the evening of November Fifth. When he landed on the road he figured they were stars. His head was buzzing and he wondered if this was really happening to him. He looked up to see the man running off behind the back of the bank. Getting to his knees he thought he'd better get off the road before any cars came. He stood up slowly and walked to the pavement.

The street was deserted, no witnesses, even though Boroughheath High Street was only twenty yards away. Chris looked in the gutter and saw the torn carrier bag. He picked it up and his eye caught the round shape of the leather night wallet which had rolled away to safety in the struggle. He picked it up, and looking around himself this time, unlocked the nightsafe, pulled open the chute, and dropped the wallet inside.

*

An hour later, sitting in Boroughheath Casualty with Amanda, Chris was watching his hands shake.

'So what did Ron do when you walked back in the shop?' she asked him.

Chris said, 'He swore a few times and asked me where the money was. He was more worried about that than me.'

Amanda had a worried look on her face and Chris knew she was close to tears. They had lived together for two years and he knew that look well.

'He's such a wimp,' she said. 'Did he call the police then?'

Chris nodded. 'By the time I'd washed my face and sat down a few minutes, a young cop about eighteen years old was there asking questions. I'm sitting in the staffroom and he's looking down at me as if he can't believe anyone would fight back. It's probably his first crime.'

'They get younger all the time.'

'He takes down all the details and says someone higher up will be in to see me on Monday.'

'You're not going to work on Monday are you?'

'I'll see how I feel.'

Chris felt lousy at that moment. Apart from the shaking hands he had a splitting headache and double vision. What had the guy hit him with, a rock? He didn't realise a fist could hit so hard. Still, the guy had hit him with fear as well.

'It's a pity no one was around,' Amanda said. 'You might've been able to catch him.'

Chris nodded. He was secretly feeling good about it as well; into the battle without a moment's hesitation. He was thinking that maybe it had something to do with his schooldays. He had played a bit of rugby back then and going in to tackle someone was second nature, something that after all these years was obviously still with him. His schooldays hadn't been a complete waste of time after all.

'Would you like another coffee?' Amanda asked.

He watched her walk over to the coffee machine. She was a tall girl, thirty-one, two years younger than him, with long dark hair. He looked at her legs and realised she was thinner than the last time he'd seen her; she was getting thinner because of him. When they'd split up a few months ago there had been some heavy scenes he never wanted to go through again. Now she was living with her father, about a mile from the YMCA where he was temporarily staying, and trying to get on without him. He had felt guilty ringing her to ask for a lift back from the hospital, but who else could he have rung? He only knew a few people in the YMCA, plus the two people he worked with in the off-licence.

Amanda came back with the coffee and handed him one.

'You'll feel better after that if you can drink it,' she said. 'Survive that, you can survive anything.' She forced a smile.

It was another fifteen minutes before Chris was called in. That made forty minutes altogether. He couldn't work out what the doctors were doing because the waiting room was virtually empty. He found that surprising for Saturday night, in this fairly rough area of suburban London. Maybe the casualties came in later when the pubs closed, and then later still there would be more from people letting off dangerous fireworks. As they sat there he could hear rockets exploding in the night sky.

Chris was placed in a small curtained cubicle and left for another twenty minutes with the curtains half closed. He watched nurses walk by in their white uniforms and black tights.

One nurse came in and asked him what was wrong. When he said he'd been mugged he felt she didn't believe him. Another one came five minutes later and asked the same question. 'I've been mugged,' Chris said again. She looked at him warily.

Eventually a doctor arrived and told him to stand up. He asked what had happened.

'I got mugged,' Chris said for the third time, trying to keep his patience.

'Let me press your face,' the doctor said. 'Tell me when it hurts.'

Chris stood there and let him press away.

'You may have a broken cheekbone,' the doctor said. He was standing so close Chris could smell his breath. Onions. 'It's starting to swell up already. In the morning it may look like a balloon. That'll mean you've got a crack somewhere and the air you're breathing is pumping it up. Like a bicycle tyre.'

Chris looked at him. Must be all of twenty three, fair hair and glasses, comparing him to a bicycle.

'You've got a graze on your cheek which means your attacker was probably wearing a ring. Your eye will be black in the morning. Don't worry about the cut lip.'

'So I just let it all heal up?'

'That's all you can do. The only problem is if infection sets in. We'll only notice that in a few weeks. Take a few days off work and you should be okay.'

'My teeth feel sore as well.'

'Go and see your dentist. Have them X-rayed.'

Chris nodded and went back out to join Amanda.

'How did it go?' she asked, still with that tearful look in her eyes.

Chris took her by the arm and led her outside. 'He compared me to a bicycle,' he said.

Amanda drove Chris the five miles back to Elmhurst where the YMCA was, asking if he wanted to go home with her first for something to eat.

'My father worries about you,' she said, 'living in that horrible place. He said to bring you home with me.'

Chris was pleased to hear that. He felt closer to Amanda's father than he did to his own.

'I couldn't eat anything if I tried,' he said. 'My jaw's too sore.'

'How about some soup?'

'No thanks.'

Chris knew Amanda had given up already because they'd passed her turning and were now approaching the YMCA entrance. He just wanted to have a couple of drinks, go to bed and sleep. He was starting to feel depressed.

Amanda turned into the YMCA entrance and drove slowly down the driveway over the sleeping policemen. The three storey building lay in front of them like a prison. It looked a depressing place to live but Chris didn't mind it. It seemed everyone else minded it more than him. Amanda parked her car in front of the reception doors.

'You don't want me to come in for a while ?' she asked.

'No. I just want a couple of whiskies and then some sleep.'

'Shall I call in tomorrow?'

'In the afternoon if you like.'

'Okay.'

Chris kissed her on the cheek and grimaced.

'Even that hurts,' he said.

'You must be in bad shape.'

He climbed out and went indoors.

Two

When Chris woke up the next day his headache had gone, but he was feeling drowsy after three stiff whiskies the previous evening. He reached out a hand to his cassette-radio, slotted in a Steve Earle tape and dozed, letting the music cheer him up. Only when he'd fully woken up, once the tape had snapped itself off, did he touch his cheek and feel something wrong.

He got out of bed and went to the mirror to have a look. He couldn't believe what he saw. It was like another person.

The left side of his face had ballooned up, making him look lopsided and foolish. He pressed it and it felt squidgy, but there wasn't anything in there except air. The doctor had been right, there must be something cracked. He was wrong about the eye though. It hadn't turned black; it was dark red instead. His lip was still swollen with a few scabs and the graze on his cheek had scabbed up too. He decided to skip shaving.

He left his ground floor room and walked down the corridor to the toilet. The toilet was ten yards away, three cubicles and a drinking water fountain. He relieved himself and got back to his room without being seen. He went back to bed, stared at the ceiling, and went through the mugging again.

Yesterday evening he had cashed up the money himself, looking through the one-way-glass into the off-licence where Ron the manager and the part-time girl Rachel were working on the till. Ron was a skiver by nature, and as he looked through the glass Chris could see him going over to a customer, talking about wine, recommending something in his posh voice, while Rachel struggled with a queue at the till. Chris had cursed, locked up the money in the wall safe, and gone to give Rachel a hand.

Chris had to do that three times while he was cashing up, and that was why he was in a bad mood when he'd left the shop; he didn't like interruptions when he was counting money, liked to get through it smoothly without any hitches. He had put the night-walleted money into one of the shop's orange carrier bags, and walked out of the front door.

On the High Street Chris had waited for a break in traffic, then crossed the road. To the left of the off-licence was the new indoor shopping mall, a fairly flash construction that wasn't bringing in enough customers yet.

Chris tried to imagine the whole of the other side of the road as he approached it. Was there anything unusual? From right to left there was Barclays Bank, then the side road, then The Plough pub, the Drop In café, and a bookies. There was a bus stop outside the pub.

Chris thought about the café. It was in an ideal place for someone to watch him from. Someone could sit in there, up near the window with a coffee, and watch him coming out of the shop every day, getting used to his routine. Maybe drinking a consoling cup of coffee after losing some money in the bookies; walking in, feeling bitter every day, sitting down watching, thinking, there goes that guy again with a carrier bag, I wonder what he's got in it? It wouldn't be too hard to figure out.

In his mind Chris had reached the other side, was walking by the bank towards the side street, looking over at The Plough on the corner. Had there been someone standing by the pub? Yes, he thought. A dark figure. Nothing more specific than that, but someone, yes.

Walking down the side road towards the nightsafe Chris hadn't bothered to look behind him to see if anyone was following. He was used to banking the money every day on his own, even though he had often told Ron that two people should go because the street was badly lit and invited trouble; the bank had just been built and suitable nightsafe lighting had been the last priority. That was the whole trouble with Boroughheath. They were rebuilding most of it, trying to turn it into a thriving town, and parts of it were still unfinished, giving the whole place the feel of a building site. Even behind the bank where the mugger had run off there was still building rubble and the Portakabin that had been a temporary bank for many months.

Chris felt his heart beating as he lay in bed. He went over it all a second time. Would he be able to recognise the person who'd been waiting by the pub and who he was willing to bet was his eventual mugger? He hadn't seen the face, it had been too dark, but maybe he would recognise the build, maybe sense something if he was standing right next to him. It was worth thinking about. He put his finger in his mouth and rubbed his sore teeth.

*

'What the hell happened to you?'

Chris was carrying his tray of Sunday roast down the canteen aisle, other residents of the YMCA looking at him. He'd decided he couldn't hide in his room all day and he'd better start getting used to the stares. He reached Bill's table and put down his tray.

'I got mugged last night.'

'No! Jesus. What happened?'

Chris told Bill the story. Bill looked at him seriously, a handsome fifty-year-old on the wrong end of two marriages, still wearing jeans and sweat shirts. Today he was wearing one that said *Le Plus Macho*.

'Well, you're some kind of hero in my book,' Bill said. 'If anyone came for me I'd say, "Here have it," and run!'

Chris smiled as he cut into his beef. 'You wouldn't have wanted them to mess up your pretty face.'

'And you shouldn't too. What made you do it?'

'I was in a bad mood, bad feelings towards the human race. If I'd been in a loving mood maybe I would've helped him, split it up later.'

'That's not a bad idea. How much was in it?'

'Under a grand in cash, a lot more in cheques and credit cards.'

'Wouldn't be worth it. Five hundred quid each.'

'Enough to take one of your girls out for a good time.'

'I don't need that much. I've got my personality to make up for cash shortages.' They both laughed, Chris finding his face still hurt when he did, but it released a bit of tension just the same.

Then Ralph came over with his tray, looked at Chris and said, 'What the fuck happened to you?'

Ralph was a long term resident at the YMCA, over a year, unemployed, killing his days in the snooker room and looking through newspapers for jobs. He was thirty-five but looked forty-five, bald down the middle of his scalp, creased up face, a younger version of Sid James without the jokes.

Chris went through the story again, with Bill interjecting a bit of spice now he knew the plot.

When he'd finished, Ralph said: 'My ex was mugged once. In Portugal. She was walking in the park with her friend one sunny afternoon when these three youngsters, teenagers they were, circled round them and took their bags. One of them had a stick. My missus started fighting back but her friend just screamed and ran away.'

'What happened to your wife?' Bill asked.

'They pushed her into some bushes and ran off. She walked out of the park looking for her friend and there she was sitting on a bench crying her eyes out. She'd pissed her pants too. Hadn't even bothered to call the cops.'

'And they never got their stuff back I bet,' Bill said.

'No. Cops couldn't do anything. My wife just lost a camera, and a tube of suntan lotion. It ruined the holiday though. She didn't talk to her friend much after that.'

Bill looked at Chris. 'I don't know anyone who's been mugged.'

'Well you do now,' Chris said.

After lunch they spent the afternoon playing snooker, a three way contest. The snooker room was on the first floor and you could usually get a game. It was no game today though because Ralph was so good.

'The amount of time you spend in here, I don't know why you don't turn professional,' Bill was saying as he lined up a shot. He became serious for a second, a model of concentration, pulled back the cue and hit hard. The cue ball hit five cushions and nothing else. They all doubled over laughing, Chris's face really hurting this time.

They played for two hours, three frames, Ralph winning them all, Chris coming second in two. He looked across the table at his friends as they played and it made him feel better. Ralph had one broken marriage, was an ex-builder without any training, and couldn't hardly write or add up. A broken face was a minor setback compared to that. And Bill was someone to look up to. He was one of the smartest people Chris had ever met, good at talking to people, working as a maintenance man in a leisure club because he'd always been too proud to sell out, put on a suit and get a so-called 'proper' job. If there was some-one he'd want to be at fifty, then Chris would be proud to be like Bill, although he wouldn't want to be living in a YMCA at that age.

As they walked back to their rooms afterwards Bill took Chris by the arm.

'If it starts to get you down just knock on my door,' he said. 'I know a lot of bad jokes. That'll cheer you up.'

Chris said thanks. He walked down the corridor to his room wondering how he could kill the rest of the day. He could either start a new paperback or drink whisky and watch TV. In his armchair he sat and thought about it for at least a minute and the whisky came out on top.

Three

Kevin Jenkins lay in bed and thought about horses. He used to think about motorways and trucks, but now it was a different kind of horse power. Well, life was all about change, wasn't it?

It was nine o'clock, Monday morning, and he could hear his father downstairs, the sound of cutlery and Breakfast TV coming up through the floor. Kevin looked at the white ceiling, took a drag on his cigarette, and blew a few smoke rings.

Every day he had to wait until his father left the house before he got up. It was annoying, but two reasons told him it was safer to stay in bed; one was Breakfast TV, and the other was they'd only start an argument. The latter would be about why Kevin didn't look harder for another job, or why he always ate with his mouth open, or why he always pumped his leg while he was sitting at the table. Both were habits Kevin never even noticed. When he ate he was a little careless, and when he sat down he couldn't keep his leg still. So what? It seemed his father couldn't start the day without an argument, before climbing into his Toyota Corolla and making his way to the post office where he was a supervisor in the Overseas Department. Kevin had worked there one Christmas a long time ago, sorting through sacks and sacks of letters, wittling them down into their prospective destinations. A month of that had been enough for him so it was no wonder his father was out for blood every morning; he'd been doing the job for thirty years.

When Kevin got out of bed he could hear the signature tune finishing Breakfast TV. He couldn't understand how his father could watch that crap every day. The presenters were so banal they just made him want to throw up, and all they talked about were babies, diets, fashion and food. And then there was that fairy that did the star signs most mornings, and finally that frizzy haired woman with the figure of an ironing board doing aerobics that left her breathless after about two minutes. Kevin couldn't understand it all. The quality of life was sinking.

Then he heard the front door shut. It was safe to leave his room.

He made his way to the bathroom and gave himself a body wash. As he wiped himself with a flannel he noticed he was getting a bit flabby now he hadn't worked for six months. When he was on the road driving trucks, it kept his arms strong and his stomach reasonably flat. Now he was getting a bit of a beer belly, and his tattooed arms had lost their muscle definition. He'd have to start doing some sit ups and press ups.

He looked at his prick hanging there and thought that looked a little shapeless too. It could do with a little work-out as well. On the road he'd been able to meet girls quite regularly but he hadn't been laid since he'd been unemployed. Still, he wasn't the only one, his old man was in the same boat. As far as Kevin knew his father hadn't been laid since his mother left three years ago. And who would want to lay him? He had lost nearly all his hair and his skin was getting that mottled look of old age. Plus he had no personality. Maybe that was why he watched Breakfast TV.

*

Kevin's local – The Coach and Horses – was on the Blackfen road, about a mile away from Boroughheath. It was open all day, but that didn't mean Kevin could afford to spend all his time in there. He couldn't see any attraction in drinking all day anyway. He turned up at his usual noon time and would stay there for the usual hour and a half.

'Hello blondie.'

This was the greeting he had to put up with every day now, since the pub had employed one Eunice Thomas, a fifty year old peroxide-blonde whose legs went up to her armpits. She always dressed in beige and Kevin liked looking at her legs as she walked up and down behind the bar, wiggling that little ass of hers, an ass a twenty-year-old would be pleased to have. It was a shame her face had aged, but one day he would take her up on that prick-teasing act of hers, get her drunk one lunchtime and go back to her place for a good going-over. Give his prick the work-out it needed.

Kevin ordered a beer and sat on a stool, the bar still quiet enough not to get jostled. It was a big pub, with the saloon bar about twice the size of the public bar. Kevin always preferred to sit in the saloon bar where Eunice served. They'd spared some expense while decorating the interior of the public bar and the clientèle it attracted was therefore rougher. Kevin had enough of a complex about being out of work not to be reminded about it every lunchtime. Today he had dressed up for Eunice in a clean pair of jeans, his favourite black leather jacket, and a thick red and green chequered shirt. On his feet he wore an old pair of Rodeo trainers, but she couldn't see his feet anyway. He pulled a newspaper out of his back pocket and spread it on the bar, open at the racing pages.

'Your lucky day today is it?' Eunice asked, placing his pint in front of him. The way she said it she could be talking about two things.

'It's always my lucky day,' Kevin said. 'If you think you're going to lose there's no point getting up, is there?'

'Seems to me you have no choice about getting up. You either do it or vegetate.'

She helped herself to the money Kevin had already placed on the bar. He watched her walk away and took a sip of beer.

After leaving the house Kevin had spent the morning in the library, like he always did. There he could read all the newspapers and study the racing comments in each. On his way to the pub he would buy a paper and then mark up his choices with a red biro, knocking back three or four pints in the process. His lunch would be a few packets of crisps and five cigarettes. As he lit one up, he saw Eunice approaching him again. He blew a cloud of smoke at her. She fanned it away with her hand and said, 'It's a bit quiet in here today. Tell me your life story.' She leaned on the counter in front of him.

Kevin drummed his fingers and wondered if she was taking the piss. When she didn't smile he reckoned she must be serious. 'You really want to know?' he asked.

'I really want to know. Surprise me.'

'There's no surprises and there's not a lot to tell. I'm only twenty-eight.'

'Well that's a start. You're twenty-eight and your name's Kevin.'

Kevin looked at her. She'd only been working in the pub a few weeks and they'd never talked much apart from flirting. They may as well get to know each other if there was an outside chance they'd end up in the sack together one day.

'Well,' Kevin said. 'I'm an unemployed driver. I've lost my licence for a year. I've been on the dole six months and I spend most of my spare time in the betting shop. Here, you want one of these?'

'Thanks,' Eunice said, taking the offered cigarette and letting Kevin light it for her. 'Do you win much?'

'Not really. I stay ahead, but I never make big amounts. It's just a game really.'

'The amount of studying you do, I thought you'd be rolling in it.'

'I might if I had the money to place. I'm not exactly bursting with cash. But I do okay. I'm just killing time.'

'The way you're always twitching I could figure that out for myself. You look like you can't wait to be somewhere else.'

'Do I twitch?'

'You're always pumping your leg.'

'You can't see my legs.'

'I can see your body shaking. You always drum your fingers too.'

'You're pretty observant.'

'It's part of my job.'

Kevin took a sip of his beer, annoyed that someone else had noticed his pumping leg. 'You enjoy it here?' he asked.

'It's okay. You meet a lot of people. How about you. Why don't you get a job?'

'Driving's all I know. I don't want to do anything else. I'll have to wait until I get my licence back.'

'How did you lose it?'

Kevin paused and took a long drag on his cigarette. He liked talking about himself. Especially to women. 'I've been driving since I was eighteen of one kind or another. I started off in removal vans. I was just a loader to start with, then I got my licence and they trained me to drive the vans. Then I got my HGV and started doing long distance stuff.'

'That's why your shoulders are so big.'

Kevin nodded. 'It's hard work driving those things. Going through small towns, reversing into awkward places.'

'So what happened?'

'I had a few days off one time between runs. Because of the money I was making, and because I was always on the move, I used to bet less frequently but in bigger amounts. One day I had a good win on a race at Newton Abbott on a horse called Out of the Gloom. Over two hundred quid. I went out to celebrate, had too much to drink, and got caught driving my dads car. Out of the Gloom plunged me right into the gloom.'

'That's bad luck.'

Kevin nodded again. 'I was not only over the limit I was driving recklessly. I was going down Lewisham High Street, a big red bus in front of me moving about two miles an hour. I pulled out to overtake and there was a traffic island right in the middle of the road. I was going too fast to pull back in so I went down the other side of the road and then pulled back in. Unfortunately a cop car saw the whole thing.'

'Well, you probably deserved it.'

'Thanks. Thing is I hardly ever drank and drove.'

'I'll be back in a minute.'

Kevin watched as Eunice went off to serve. He wouldn't tell her the bit about when he'd arrived back home at his dad's place after being caught. After telling his old man what had happened, the smell of drink still on his breath, they'd entered into a very loud argument. Kevin had lost his temper, had really flipped if he had to be honest about it, and had grabbed his dad in the hallway by the throat. He'd had him pushed up against the wall ready to throttle when there'd been a banging on the front door. The local bobby on his beat had heard the argument from the street and had stopped to make sure everything was okay. Kevin's father had told the cop it was all right, the cop not believing him at all. Kevin had been lucky not to be arrested. It made him shudder to think what would've happened if the cop hadn't arrived. Would he have cooled down in time before the fists started flying? He knew he had a temper but that was one of the few times it had erupted on a person.

Eunice returned to his end of the bar. Kevin had managed to circle a few horses while she'd been away. 'So you get your licence back in another six months?' she asked.

'Yeah. Roll on six months.'

'Are you married?'

'No. I live with my dad. I decided to move back with him for the duration. I can't afford rented digs at the moment.' Kevin shrugged. 'We put up with each other.' When Kevin had lost his licence it had been his father's suggestion to move back in with him. Even after that argument. The old man must be the forgiving type.

'And where's your mother?' Eunice asked.

'She left three years ago.'

'So you're looking for a mother figure?'

Kevin grinned. 'Maybe I am.' He finished his beer and gave Eunice his glass. 'Another of these and then you can tell me your life story.'

*

It was a quick bus ride to Boroughheath and the betting shop in the High Street. Kevin left at half-one so he could get a bet on the two o'clock race. He was in a good mood after his chat with Eunice, especially after finding out she lived alone. She was divorced (everyone seemed to be these days) and had a whole flat to herself as part of the settlement. Her ex-husband was an engineer who had gone into a second childhood. Now he was single again, he could hang out in pubs and talk about sport with his cronies. As far as women were concerned he wasn't interested, hadn't had an affair since they'd split up five years ago. Kevin couldn't figure that one out. He couldn't ever see a day when he wouldn't be after one woman or another.

The bus stopped right outside the bookies and Kevin pushed open the door and walked into the smoky atmosphere. He loved it. The carpet was bright green giving the impression of walking on turf, and halfway down the right there were TV sets, about ten of them, showing runners and riders, and odds on other sports should the races not be going your way. Kevin kept to racing during the week unless there was a big fight on, cup football, or snooker. It added a bit of variety. Now, he walked up to the window, said hello to Mickey who was always there, and placed his bet on the first race at Newmarket, getting that out of the way so he could relax for the next ten minutes. Then he took his paper, leaned on a ledge, and waited for it all to begin. He wondered where Dashy was.

When the race got under way Dashy walked in, nodded at Kevin, and walked hurriedly up to the window. He was too late to place a bet. He swore and came over to Kevin.

'Good start to the day,' Dashy said. 'Got caught up in the pub. Chatting up women. Didn't get anywhere though.' He smirked at his bad luck. Dashy's real name was Leo Dash but everyone called him Dashy. Kevin thought that highly original.

'That's usually the way,' Kevin said.

'Turned out to be a waste of time.'

'Let's listen to the race.'

Kevin looked up at the TV screens and listened to the commentary. Dashy shuffled beside him, looking at a newspaper, getting ready for the next race. Kevin felt himself getting tense as the race neared its end. He'd bet on a horse to place but it came in fifth. A poor start to the afternoon.

'Let's try again,' he said to Dashy, and they went up to Mickey and laid some more money down.

'So how was your weekend?' Kevin asked Dashy when they were back leaning against the wall.

'Didn't win anything on the football. Didn't even get close.'

'That's tough.'

Dashy had never won anything on football as far as Kevin could remember, and he wondered where he got his money from. Okay, so he won a few times on the horses, but there was no way he stayed ahead. And he was only on the dole, just like him.

Kevin had teamed up with Dashy a few months before, after he'd first noticed him as a bookies regular. Before that he'd mixed with a few older men, most of them retired or on their way there, and it was a change to have someone his own age, or thereabouts, to talk to.

Dashy was just over six feet tall, had broad sloping shoulders, short dark curly hair, and a strong looking physique. Kevin wouldn't fancy his chances in a fight with him, partly because of Dashy's build, partly because he was that bull headed type of a guy who would fight without caring about the consequences. He would wave fists and feet, take as good as he got, and worry about the injuries later. Some days Dashy came in with a black eye or a cut lip and would explain it away as 'a fight up the pub.' He'd had so many 'fights up the pub' Kevin reckoned he must be banned from just about everywhere. It was a subject he didn't press, and he confined their friendship just to the bookies. Dashy had asked him out drinking often enough, but Kevin was smart enough to get out of it every time.

'Got another tattoo done on Saturday,' Dashy said. He pulled his pullover and T-shirt out of his jeans. There was a red and blue mess on his stomach.

'What the fuck's that?' Kevin asked.

'It'll be a bat when it dries up.'

'What do you want a bat for?'

'Well, who else has got one?'

'Batman?'

The first time Dashy had spoken to Kevin it had been about tattoos. Kevin had been standing with his sleeves rolled up, the tattoos on his forearms highly visible. Dashy had spent the next ten minutes showing all of his to Kevin. He had a lizard on his forearm and his back was a blue and red illustration of snakes, eagles, naked women, and a few other things, all concocted together in what Dashy called 'a work of art.' Kevin was alarmed to see this was now spreading to his stomach.

'What do girls say when they see all this?' he asked.

'They're shocked at first,' Dashy laughed. 'But then they get used to it. Turns 'em on.'

'Yeah?'

Kevin didn't believe it for a minute. As far as he knew Dashy didn't even have a girlfriend. He didn't look the type of bloke who'd pull much either. That curly hair would put most girls off. It looked as though a clump of pubic hair had been placed on his head. And it was turning grey already too. And if Kevin had tattoos like that he'd keep his shirt on all the time. He liked the ones on his own arms but that was as far as he would let them spread.

They listened to the commentary again as the next race came on. Kevin listened in silence, while Dashy swore out loud next to him. Sometimes Dashy was embarrassing to be with, but Kevin couldn't imagine a whole day in the bookies without someone to talk to. Most days Dashy was better than nothing.

When the race finished Kevin picked up his five pounds win and Dashy sulked. They placed their next bet and went out to the street.

'I've got to go to the office,' Kevin said, and they crossed the road, heading for the Shopping Mall. 'The office' as Kevin called it, was the Gents. It was the cleanest Gents in town – a quick ride up to the second floor in the elevator – and the nearest to the bookies. There was usually an attendant in there, but today it was empty. As Kevin stood washing his hands afterwards, Dashy leant on a sink telling a joke.

'There was this man driving along the street in his mini, and in the back he's got a load of penguins just sitting there. He gets pulled over by a cop and the cop says to him…'

Dashy stopped telling his joke when the Gents door opened and a small skinny guy came in. Dashy fumbled in his pocket for a cigarette, looking uneasy all of a sudden, and watched as the man went to the urinal. Kevin looked in the mirror at the man. He knew him from somewhere. He'd never known Dashy to stop mid-joke before.

'So the cop says to him,' Kevin continued for him, 'why are you driving along with all those penguins in your car? I've heard it before.' He dried his hands and looked at Dashy who was still looking at the man. 'Lets go,' he said.

When they were back down on the shopping level Kevin noticed Dashy relaxing again. They walked along the brightly lit walkway, idly looking in shop windows, not really taking much of an interest. Dashy was always more interested in the security guards, seeing if there was anyone new on the beat, seeing if they looked tough, seeing if they looked tougher than him. This game always amused Kevin. He would walk beside Dashy and watch him giving a guard the eye as they walked past. Trying to stare them out. Kevin didn't fancy any of their chances against Dashy and would love to see a fight or two, but Dashy wasn't the type to get involved in mid-afternoon in front of a load of shoppers. At night time after a few drinks was more his style.

'Look at those beefcakes!' Dashy said, as they walked past two guards chatting up a group of teenage girls. One of them was short and fit looking, standing there cracking his knuckles, legs apart in a bow legged stance. The other was well over six feet, cropped hair and black beard, his gut straining the buttons on his jacket.

'Little and Large,' Dashy laughed. 'You wouldn't catch me in one of those outfits!'

He'd said that pretty loud and Kevin was worried when the big one glanced over at them. He grabbed Dashy's arm and pulled him along, looking back at the guards posing in their crimson jackets and black trousers.

They walked to the central fountains where there were fake marble seats and plastic plants. They lit cigarettes and sat and smoked. Kevin was still trying to think who the man in the toilet had been. He recognised the face, but couldn't put a name to it. Then he got it. He was one of the guys who worked in the off-licence down the road. Turn right out of the Shopping Mall, and about three shops down. Small, rattish looking runt always giving orders in there; a bit of a phony. Him and Dashy often went in during the afternoon to buy a few cans. Take them on to the street and drink between races. So why was Dashy acting so uncomfortable about it?

Kevin noticed he was pumping his leg again but he didn't bother stopping because Dashy was the only person never to complain about it. Probably didn't even notice. Kevin looked at him sitting there deep in thought, a big aggressive bear whose only interests were beer, women, betting, and tattoos. He felt a bit sorry for him. Would Dashy ever work again? Who would take the risk of employing someone like him? Even the jobs he'd done in the past, building labourer and factory work, were getting scarce. He reckoned Dashy had a long, hard life in front of him and there was nothing he'd be able to do about it. Twenty-five and he may never work again. Still, Kevin had enough problems of his own. He yawned; the midday drinking was getting to him.

'Let's get back to the bookies,' he said, nudging Dashy in the ribs.

As they walked out of the Mall on to the High Street, Kevin stopped and said, 'Fancy getting some cans?' He looked at Dashy, who squirmed again, the way he'd done in the Gents.

'No, I'm not thirsty,' he said. He was looking the other way, off down the road, the opposite direction to where the off-licence was.

'Well, I'm going to get one,' Kevin said. He didn't really want a beer, just wanted to see what was up with Dashy.

'I'll wait here. I'll look at the stereos.' Kevin watched Dashy walk to Lasky's window, shrugged his shoulders and went into the off-licence.

Inside The Wine Seller, Kevin pulled a can of Carlsberg Special Brew off a stack in the middle of the floor and paid at the till. The tasty young girl assistant was serving, and she gave him a reluctant smile. Kevin went back on the street, tugged off the ring pull and looked at Dashy as he sauntered back to him sipping on his beer. Lasky's window had obviously lost interest for Dashy because now he was standing there, waiting. Looking at him.

'Want a sip?' Kevin asked, holding out the can.

Dashy took it, sipped, and handed it back.

'Listen,' Dashy said. 'Can you keep a secret?'

'Of course,' Kevin said. Now they were getting to it.

'Let's go over here and I'll tell you.'

They stood at the curb waiting for the traffic to ease. Dashy looked at the passing cars, staring vacantly as if he were about to throw himself under one of them.

Then he turned to Kevin. 'I got into a bit of trouble on Saturday night,' he said.

Four

Chris and Bill were walking back to the YMCA. They had just done a quick tour of Elmhurst village, the short High Street with its few shops and pubs, one supermarket, and two garages. Although Elmhurst was only five miles from Boroughheath, it couldn't be more different; this was a respectable commuter area with a country atmosphere, expensive homes and a low crime rate. There were seven pubs in the general area and nearly as many antique shops. If you needed to buy anything that wasn't food or expensive clothes, then you would have to hop on a bus to either Bromley or Boroughheath and their new shopping malls. It was Tuesday morning and although the swelling had gone down a little, the walk in the cold air was making Chris's face ache.

'The only thing I don't like about living in the YMCA,' Chris was saying, 'is that you have to be out of your room by eight every day. How am I meant to get a lie-in during the week?'

'You're not,' Bill said. 'They assume most people work Monday to Friday.'

'It's all right for you.'

'Not really. I get to the health club late some days. I mean, here I am killing time with you.'

Chris looked at his watch. 'If we slow down a bit they'll be finished by the time we get back.' He shivered. 'On days like these I'd rather make my own bed and clean my room myself. It would take me five minutes. We're turfed out for over an hour.'

'Rules are rules.'

'You said it.' Chris looked at the passing cars but couldn't make out if people were looking at his face. From a distance he probably looked normal.

'It's okay for the money,' Bill said. 'Sixty-two quid a week and all the stodge you can eat.'

'And warm rooms.'

'You know, if you stay there a long time your rent goes down? Discount for long service.'

'I'll be out as soon as I can,' Chris said. 'I miss my lie-ins.'

They turned the corner and the YMCA came into view. On their left was a high wire fence, then the half-size football field, then the red-bricked YMCA. It had a flat roof and the rough shape of two E's stuck back to back.

'Not a welcoming sight, is it?' Chris said.

'No,' Bill said. 'But Liz is.' He was looking ahead at a blonde girl waiting at the bus stop outside the YMCA gates. Chris recognised the girl; she was there some mornings when he caught the bus to work. Now she was looking at Bill, smiling, and said hello to him as they approached.

'Out for your morning walk?' she asked.

'Just exercising the injured here,' Bill said. 'This is Chris. He doesn't always look like this.'

Chris reached out and shook Liz's gloved hand. He felt a fool with his swollen face.

'I've seen you here before,' he said.

'But you never talk to me.'

Chris shrugged. 'Who ever talks in the morning?'

'Well, you'll be able to talk in the future,' Bill said. Chris looked at him.

'What happened to your face?' Liz asked.

Chris went through the story again, this time giving an edited version because he was sick of telling it. He stood with the swollen part of his face away from Liz. He liked the way she listened to him, attentive, not letting her eyes wander off. He liked her blonde hair too, cut short, although he could see some dark roots showing through. She was smartly dressed but with a little too much make up for his liking. When he'd finished his story she looked impressed.

'Well, if I ever need protecting on a dark street I'll know who to call,' she said. Chris smiled.

'Here comes your bus,' Bill said.

They watched Liz climb on and waved goodbye. They walked down the drive to the YMCA.

'You're just an old smoothy, Bill, you know that? How come you know every girl in town?'

'I talk to them. You've got to show interest.'

'Had any luck with Liz?'

'No. I've been trying to get her to come to the health club. Take her for a swim, or a work out in the gym. Loosen her up a little. Finish off with a few drinks in the bar.'

'Then maybe the sun bed or a quick massage?'

'You get the picture.'

'I think she's too young for you.'

'She's a lot younger than you too. Twenty-five, I think. You want her, you can have her. I've got a million others to work on.'

'Because you talk to them?'

When they reached the YMCA reception area they sat down on a couple of armchairs. The foyer had two pay phones, eight brown armchairs, and three noticeboards with house rules and local events stuck on them. To the left of the main door was the reception cubby hole, and next to that a door that led to the offices and the manager's apartment.

'Let's give it another five minutes,' Bill said, looking at his watch and lighting up a cigarette.

Chris didn't smoke so he sat and looked at his hands. There were a few other residents waiting for their rooms to be finished. Most of the residents were employees of the Ministry of Defence, apprentices who were learning how to build missiles or something in a factory down the road. They were loud teenagers who Chris didn't bother mixing with. The rest of the residents were people like himself, Bill, and Ralph, ordinary citizens, temporarily homeless or down on their luck. Chris mixed with them because they had something in common – their momentary exclusion from mainstream life.

'So how did your police visit go?' Bill asked Chris.

'Okay. He was a nice bloke.'

Chris had been visited by a plainclothes policeman the previous morning, a tall chap with a drooping black moustache.

'He reminded me of Dennis Weaver,' Chris said. 'You remember that cop show *McCloud*? He took down a detailed statement, and gave me some tips for the future.'

'On what, how to live your life? How to chat up girls? You need a few of those.'

'On how to carry a night wallet.' Chris stood up, ready to act it out.

'Now here's what you do,' he said. 'You carry an empty carrier bag, or rather, not empty, you put something worthless in it.'

'Like your dirty laundry?'

'Yeah, something like that. Then you put the night wallet

with the money inside your coat and under your armpit. Wedge it in like this.' Chris demonstrated.

'You'd have to get the wallets fumigated after about a month.'

'Then you walk along looking natural...' Chris strutted down the foyer, the other residents looking at him as if he were mad.

'I couldn't look natural with a lump under my arm,' Bill said.

'And when you come to the nightsafe you do this.' Chris was up against the wall now, grinning. 'You hold the carrier up and make it look as though you're taking something out. Then instead, you slip the sweaty wallet from under your armpit, and slot it into the nightsafe.'

Bill looked at him bemused. 'So what's the deal with the carrier bag?'

Chris gave him a impatient look. 'If you're walking along with the carrier bag swinging by your side and the mugger runs up and grabs it, what does he get?'

Bill raised a finger. 'I'm with you.'

'Good.' Chris sat down and laughed.

'Our rooms should be ready by now,' Bill said. 'I've got to go. Thanks for the lesson in personal security.'

*

'I don't know why the hospital didn't X-ray your cheek,' Mr Bicker was saying. 'They've got the equipment, of course they have. Maybe they were busy. I can only do your teeth.'

Chris looked up at the chubby dentist probing away in his mouth. He couldn't reply with about three fingers stuck in there.

'You've got a loose tooth here at the back. Nothing serious. And a bit's been chipped off another one here. The loose one will grow back in again. The chipped one we'll leave.'

Chris relaxed as the fingers came out of his mouth. Bicker was the friendliest dentist he'd ever had and also the only doctor he trusted. The man had knowledge.

'Let's get you X-rayed,' Bicker said as he washed his hands. 'I'll leave you with nurse Roberts.'

Chris smiled at the middle aged nurse as he stood up. They went into another room and she put something in his mouth before she started X-raying. Then Chris sat in the waiting room until the results came through.

'Well, I can't see any fracture,' Mr Bicker said, holding the X-ray in his hand. They were standing in the corridor now, away from prying eyes in the waiting room. 'There's a dark line down here,' he said, running a chubby finger down Chris's cheek, 'but that could just be a root showing up. I can't really tell. Let's just leave it a few weeks, and if you start getting headaches or anything feels wrong, come back and see me straight away.'

Chris thanked him, and went down to the street feeling reassured.

He spent an hour walking around Bromley looking in shops and avoiding people's stares. The swelling in his face was going down but he was still a long way from looking normal. Being around so many people again was also starting to give him a feeling of paranoia. If he heard someone running up behind him he would automatically flinch, expecting to be hit. When he saw groups of noisy kids loitering outside shops he just wanted them to say something to him, pick on him once, so he could lay a few of them out. The feeling of wanting revenge was rearing its ugly head and any excuse to hit someone would be the ideal outlet. At the same time he knew that another punch on his head could really do some damage, loosen all those parts that were still holding together so far. He thought he'd better hold back until he was properly healed up again and feeling strong.

*

By Wednesday morning Chris had decided to go back to work. He was bored with sitting in his room all day and felt it was time to meet the world again, get used to facing people with a swollen mug. As he walked to the bus stop he saw Liz standing there, waiting.

'Hi!' she said as he walked up. 'Returning to the land of the living?'

Chris nodded towards the YMCA. 'I'm tired of being cooped up in there. It's driving me crazy.'

'Is it that bad?'

'It's like living in a one-star hotel. It's okay but it's very quiet during the day. Everyone's at work.'

'Well, they're meant to be.'

'That's right. Where do you live?'

Liz pointed behind Chris to a turning off the main road. 'Just down there. Just a two minute walk. I get the bus to Sidcup and then a train into London.'

'What do you do up there?'

'I work for a film company in the West End.'

'Sounds glamourous.'

'Not really, I'm just a secretary. It'll lead to other things though. I want to meet some famous people.'

Chris nodded. He tried to think of a famous person he'd like to meet.

'I'd like to meet Jamie Lee Curtis,' he said.

Liz laughed. 'Wouldn't most men?'

Chris couldn't think of anything else to say. He was out of practice when it came to chatting up women. The only female he'd talked to since splitting up with Amanda was Rachel at work.

'I get a lot of free film tickets,' Liz said then. 'If I get any for Jamie Lee Curtis films I'll let you have one.'

'Thanks. I liked her in *A Fish Called Wanda*. I don't think I've seen her in anything since, though.'

'I could've got you a ticket for that.'

Again the conversation stopped. If Bill could see him now, Chris thought, he'd say he wasn't doing too well. Chris put it down to the fact that Liz wasn't really his type. She was a definite yuppie, although he had to admit she was a very good looking one. Even out here in the cold, waiting for the bus with her big grey coat hiding her figure.

'Here comes my bus,' Liz said. 'Will you be here tomorrow?'

'Should be,' Chris said, relaxing.

'I'll see you then.'

Chris watched as Liz climbed on the bus, and looked at her legs in black stockings and high-heeled shoes. He watched her walking the length of the double decker and then sitting by the window on his side. She smiled at him as the bus pulled away. Maybe he hadn't done so badly after all.

*

When Chris walked up to The Wine Seller off-licence, Rachel was waiting outside the front door. She gave him a big happy smile and asked how he was. He fumbled in his pocket for his keys.

'Better for seeing your smiling face,' he said.

He pushed open the door and the alarm went off, a shrill, piercing bell. He walked quickly to the back of the shop and silenced it before it blew his head off. He hated being greeted by that noise every day.

They went into the staffroom and started making cups of tea.

'You've been working full-time while I've been away?' Chris asked.

'Yes. I need all the money I can get. It's nice to have you back but I hope Ron doesn't send me home.'

'I'll ask him not to.'

'Thanks.'

Chris liked being back with Rachel. She was a saucy little seventeen-year-old with short brown hair. She was a Madonna fan and liked gelling her hair every which way but normal, acquiring a different look nearly every day.

They sat down with their tea and Chris explained his injuries, Rachel looking at him like he was a normal person, like there really wasn't a bulge on his cheek and a red mark under his eye. He was having a hard time keeping his eyes on her face. No matter how cold it was Rachel always came to work in short skirts, usually denim, with no tights on underneath. Her legs weren't the greatest in the world but he still found them very appealing, the skirt sliding its way up her thigh as she sat there listening. Chris had often thought about asking her out. They'd been working together a year and he'd managed to hold off so far. He knew his motives were mainly carnal and once the quick fling was over they'd still have to work together. It wouldn't be worth the trouble. Maybe when one of them left. That would be the time to do it.

'And what did the police say?' Rachel asked.

'They said there's virtually no chance of catching the bloke unless he does it again somewhere.'

Chris could remember another time they'd been together in the staffroom. Rachel had been making the tea but had spilt some down the front of her white blouse. She'd been standing at the sink wiping off the tea with a cloth and had then been left with a soaking wet blouse. She'd untucked it from her skirt and knelt in front of the fan heater on the floor drying it. Chris had been sitting watching, or rather trying not to watch, the blouse blowing up above Rachel's waist showing off her bare stomach. She'd known the effect she was having too, had played the scene out as long as possible.

'Well, it's good to have you back,' Rachel said, just as Ron walked in.

'Thought I heard voices,' Ron said. 'Thought Rachel was going mad. How are you Chris?' He stood there in his shirt and tie and a smart pair of grey trousers. Always Mister Neat, Chris thought. Always wears nice clothes because he knows he won't be getting them dirty.

Chris went through it all again. Ron listened as he made himself a strong cup of coffee and lit a cigarette. Ron drank about fifteen cups of coffee every day and smoked as many cigarettes. Chris dreaded to think what his insides must look like.

Ron was only about five-six, a skinny little guy with bowed legs. His face was all points: nose, chin, ears, and hair. The hair was short and black and stuck straight up as if he'd just had a fright. With his pointed nose he reminded Chris of a rat. And the way he walked too. Short quick bursts, as if a cat were after him. Despite all these shortcomings he had managed to find himself quite an attractive wife, a girl with wealthy parents who had seen them into a comfortable home. The home was the only thing Chris envied about him.

Chris came to the end of his story and Ron said, 'Well, you're better now, that's the main thing.' He looked at his watch. 'Shit! We'd better open up. What will the customers think?'

*

When his lunchbreak came around, Chris went out for a newspaper. He hated buying one in the Shopping Mall and always went to a small newsagent a bit further down the road. He liked giving business to smaller shops. He hated the indoor malls that were sprouting up all over the country, making big companies richer and killing off many family businesses. And what purpose did they serve anyway? They all had about twenty shoe shops, twenty jewellery shops, and nothing else. Chris was glad his off-licence was part of a small chain. The day he had to work for the likes of Victoria Wine would be the day he'd give up.

Walking back with his paper Chris looked over the other side of the road and saw the bookies. Mecca. It was a modern building which looked more like an estate agents, except that the windows were painted green. Thinking back to his flimsy theory about his mugger, Chris decided to go in and have a look. He waited for the lights and crossed the road.

Chris had been in a bookies only a few times in his life, placing bets on big races like the Grand National and the Derby. Betting held no fascination for him, but he did like watching sport on TV, and went to see Crystal Palace a couple of times a season. He pushed open the door and went in.

He was expecting to find a squalid little place, but was surprised to find green carpet and TV screens up on the walls. The place was almost clean, except for the clouds of cigarette smoke and the resultant ash on the floor. He walked up to the screens and stood there, watching.

Most of the TVs were filled with racing bets, races about to get under way, or races just finished all over the country, displayed in bright lettering. On one screen were the odds for that night's football matches. Chris went over to a screen at the side and by pressing an index button was given a choice of screens he could look at. He pressed a few of them and looked at odds on a snooker tournament and a Frank Bruno fight. He didn't realise you could place so many different kinds of bets – football scorelines, or how many rounds a fight would last. He could quite easily get into this if he had the money to burn.

He leaned on the wall in front of the screens and looked around at the other men there. Most of them were old and retired, probably single, waiting out the rest of their days. There were a few Chris's age, maybe slightly older, but not that many younger. They all looked pretty rough to Chris, the kind of person you wouldn't want to get in an argument with down the pub on a Saturday night, the type of person he'd see at football matches; the swagger of violence, the type who turned into a stumbling psychopath after a few beers. Chris couldn't see anyone who looked vaguely like his mugger, so he walked towards the door, thinking maybe he was being foolish.

The door opened just before he got to it though, and two young guys walked in, smelling of beer. He stood back to let them in, and the dark one, coming in second, gave him a funny look. Chris felt something sliding down his back, a tingling feeling, one he didn't like. He watched the two walk past, watched the way the dark one walked. He couldn't be sure about anything, and walked out on to the street.

He stood at the curb waiting for the traffic to break and he could feel the sweat running down his back.

Five

When Kevin turned away from the betting window, Dashy pulled him over to the side with a worried look on his face. Kevin asked him what was up.

'That was him!' Dashy said. 'That was the bloke!'

'That was what bloke? What are we talking about?' Kevin noticed the sweat on Dashy's forehead, and his eyes were darting around like a madman's. He'd also turned white, and was still gripping on to his arm. 'Let go, will you? You're squeezing me to death.'

'Sorry.' Dashy let go. 'The bloke we just walked past coming in?' He lowered his voice. 'That was the one I went after Saturday night.'

'What the hell was he doing in here?'

'How the fuck do I know? Maybe he recognised me, knows who I am.'

'If he does, you're in trouble. Stay away from me!' Kevin moved away and started laughing. Dashy didn't find it amusing. He grabbed him by the arm again and pulled him up close.

'This isn't a joke,' he whispered. 'I may be in deep shit. You've got to help me.'

'All right, all right. Just let go of my arm.' Kevin prised himself loose again. 'Let's get out of here. People are starting to look at us.'

They walked outside and turned left down the side street where the nightsafe was. Further on was a car park and that had been the place on Monday where Dashy had told Kevin about the mugging. Standing there amongst the cars. Kevin hadn't believed him at first, had known Dashy was dumb, but not dumb enough to do that. Then he'd caught the despair in his voice and the way Dashy was acting so nervous. Now he was nervous again. Standing amongst the cars. Kevin tried to calm him down.

'Have you ever seen him in the bookies before?' he asked.

'Never. He doesn't go in there. You can tell he's not a punter.'

'How do you tell that?'

'He's too neat. We're all scruffs in there.'

Kevin laughed. 'Come on! You get the occasional suit walking in. Anyway, he's not so neat. Shirt and trousers. You think that's neat? You should go to the City, have a look around up there.'

'What the fuck would I want to go there for?'

'No reason. Just see some neat people. I was driving my truck through there once. I was passing Cannon Street tube when this swarm of suits came out of the station and headed across the road. I had to ram on the brakes to keep from running them over. You wouldn't believe it! They walk off the trains, through the station, and right over the road without stopping. Hold up all the traffic as if they have right of way! It's like a fucking army. Or a swarm more like. And what's more, they have these photo shops where they all queue up for their holiday snaps. You've never seen so many tans. And…'

Dashy was looking at him. 'What the fuck're you telling me this for?'

'I'm trying to calm you down. Get your mind off it.'

'Well you're not succeeding. You're just winding me up!'

'Okay, okay.' Kevin backed away. He was enjoying his moment of power, seeing Dashy squirm a bit. Teach him to go out mugging people. He pulled out his cigarettes and offered him one. They lit up and leaned on a car.

'Now what makes you think he knows you?' Kevin asked.

Dashy moaned. 'Well, why was he there? He's never been there before! For fucks sake.'

'Maybe he's trying to work things out. Maybe he's figured out your plan. It wouldn't be too hard, would it?'

'What do you mean?'

'Okay. He says to himself – I've been mugged.' Kevin paused. 'He says – my attacker must've been watching me from somewhere to get to know my routine. Unless it was just a spur of the moment thing, which can't be dismissed because you made such a hash of it.'

'Don't push it.'

'So he thinks – where would he be watching me from? The pub next to the side road? No. The windows are all coloured glass. Can't see a thing out of there. He'd have to stand on a seat to look out. Bit obvious if you're in the pub eh?'

'Ha, ha.'

'So he thinks – the cafe next to the pub. Now there's an ideal place to watch from. And he wouldn't be wrong, would he?'

'And then what does he think?'

'I don't know. He thinks that's where you were so he starts looking in the places around it. Tries to get into the mind of the criminal.'

Dashy nodded.

'He's going over things, that's all. He doesn't know fuck all. But he will if you start acting odd.'

Dashy was silent.

'Just play it cool. If he comes in again just act normal. Go about your betting. Soon he'll get tired of the place and try somewhere else. He'll go to the pub and start standing on seats!'

Dashy smiled at last.

'Just take it easy,' Kevin said. 'Now let's go back and see if I've won any money.'

*

Kevin's words had helped at the time, but as he was walking home Dashy started to worry again. Now he was on his own, letting his imagination work, things didn't seem so rosy.

He was sure that bastard knew about him.

But what could he do about it?

Knock him off?

He was so skint he didn't even have enough to go to the pub. That would mean missing out on Helen. She was the reason he'd tried the mugging in the first place, so he could take her out sometime and impress her. Now some other bastard would move in.

He'd first seen Helen about a month ago. She'd been with a group of greasers and had been a greasy-looking girl herself; long, dirty black hair, black leather jacket, and dirty denims. Dashy had never liked that type of crowd, coming into the pub carrying their helmets, piling them up in a corner, smoking roll-ups, smelling of bike. He'd always thought it an act, a big phony come-on – here I am the tough Brando biker, you'd better not fool with me! He knew he could knock any of them over with one quick punch.

After that first sighting Dashy hadn't seen Helen for about a week, and then she came in with a group of girls one night and she looked *clean*. The leather jacket had gone, her hair had been

shampooed, and now she wore stone-washed jeans and cow-
boy boots. He'd talked to her most of the evening, after his
mates had decided to muscle in on the group; sitting next to
her trying to keep track of the conversation, all the time trying
not to look down the front of her blue denim shirt. He'd been
excited by that. Could see there was a lot of breast under there
waiting to spring out. Two big handfuls.

When Helen had asked him what he did for a living, Dashy
had said he was a professional gambler! He couldn't tell her he
was on the dole, so he'd told her he just spent his time in the
bookies and made money that way, which was partly true
because that's all he did. He asked her if she'd ever seen that
old TV programme called *Big Deal*. She said yes, once or twice,
and he said, well I'm like the hero of that, Robbie Box, a professional gambler. She'd been impressed with that. He could see it
in her eyes. Here she was down the pub with her girlfriends, a
quiet midweek evening, sitting next to a real character, a gambler who may have fingers in other pies. Wasn't it exciting! For
the first time in months Dashy had started liking himself again.

But after they'd met up a few more times, Dashy could see
Helen wasn't as dumb as all that. She had reverted to her biker
friends and seemed to be getting bored with him and his bull-
shitting ways. So what he'd really needed was a big score so he
could take her out and impress her, really show her what a big
timer he was. That's when he'd started thinking about robbery,
the only way to get some big money quickly.

Now, walking home, it seemed everything was turning sour.
He'd bungled the robbery, the guy he'd mugged might be on to
him, and he'd lose out on Helen if he didn't impress her quickly.

Dashy fished in his pocket for his front door keys, and let
himself into his parents' semi-detached. He went silently up to
his room and lay down on the bed.

He closed his eyes and immediately felt sleepy. He thought
about Helen and her tits and started to get a hard on. He'd just
got his hands down his jeans when the door opened and his
mother walked in. He quickly yanked his hand out but was still
lying there with his flies undone.

'I thought you'd come in, Leo,' his mother said. 'Don't you
say hello anymore?'

'I feel tired,' Dashy said. 'Got a lot on my mind.'

'I'm surprised you've still got a mind the amount of use you put it to,' she joked. She came and sat on the edge of the bed. Dashy looked up at her. She was in her mid-forties and starting to wrinkle up. She used too much make-up, and had her hair dyed a different shade of red every time she went to the hairdressers. He saw her looking at his undone flies. 'Have you got a stomach ache?'

'Yeah. I feel bloated,' he lied.

'There's something else wrong too, isn't there?'

'No,' Dashy said. 'I'm right as rain.'

'It hasn't rained for weeks though.'

They sat and looked at each other and she asked him for the umpteenth time if he wanted his room decorated to cheer him up. Dashy looked at the walls. They were painted red and were covered with colour magazine pictures of famous sportsmen, most of them players from The Arsenal. That's why the walls were red. He'd had it painted this colour when he was a teenager, when he and his younger brother Danny had been mad on football. They'd wanted red and white, the Arsenal strip, but their dad had told them to stop being bloody silly. Now Danny was dead, a suicide at fifteen, and Dashy liked to keep the room like this in memory of him...

Dashy had been the one, eight months before, to find Danny dead, hung by his own belt in the small back garden shed. They had grown up together in this same bedroom – Danny's bed was still there, pushed up against the wall – and Dashy had thought he knew his younger brother almost as well as he knew himself. Okay, so Danny had threatened suicide on a number of occasions, but he'd never taken him seriously; young kids were always saying such things.

Then one evening after work, Dashy had been the first one home and had seen the shed door open from the kitchen window. He'd walked down to the shed, expecting to see Danny working on his bike, and had instead found him hanging from the roof, dead, suffocated by his belt, as the pathologist had said later.

Dashy had taken a week off work, he'd been so upset. Then the day he returned to work, he had got in an argument with the foreman, a short Scottish wanker called Angus. Dashy had laid him out with a single punch, been sacked on the spot, and had been on the dole ever since.

Danny's death had been reported in the local newspaper, and for some weeks the family's friends had stayed clear, as if they'd been to blame for his death. And maybe they had been. Dashy didn't know. He still had the newspaper cutting somewhere which ended with the coroners quote: 'I can only record an open verdict on the sad and tragic death of this little boy.' Dashy felt those words would haunt him for the rest of his life. He looked at his mother who was tut-tutting at his room.

'No, I like it like this,' he said.

'But it's so messy.'

'It's got character.'

Most of the pictures on the walls were so old they were nearly falling off. The Sellotape had turned brown, and there where yellow undercoat marks where Dashy had ripped off pictures of Arsenal players who'd been transferred. Apart from the footballers there were old pictures of other sporting greats like Borg, Connors, Ali, Nicklaus, and Ovett. How many rooms in Britain had pictures like those?

'I like it like this,' Dashy said again.

His mother sighed and told him supper would be ready in half an hour. She left the room.

Dashy didn't feel sleepy anymore or turned-on by Helen. Just depressed. He'd have to spend the evening watching TV with his parents. His father would sit in front of the TV stroking his black beard, neither moving nor talking for the whole evening. Since Danny's death he had grown more and more morose, and to add to it, his job as manager of an electrical shop was now in danger. The shop – called Bright Sparks – was down the wrong end of Boroughheath High Street and had suffered since the new shopping mall had opened. If the shop went under the owner could always sell the building for a tidy sum, but where would that leave Dashy's dad? On the dole at the age of forty-eight and lucky to find another job. Dashy reluctantly admitted his father had a right to feel morose. What a fucked-up family they made.

He stood up, zipped his jeans, and went downstairs. On the way down he realised that *Sportsnight* would be on later. There was something to look forward to after all.

*

The next morning Dashy got up early to catch his father before he went to work. He went downstairs in his dressing gown and greeted him at the kitchen table. Thankfully his mother was upstairs in the bathroom. Dashy said good morning to him.

'A good game last night, wasn't it?' Dashy said.

'Not as good as it used to be,' his father said, not looking up from his newspaper.

'Why not?' Dashy asked, already disappointed with his fathers depressed tone.

'There's too much money in the game. The players are spoilt and the administration are idiots.'

'What do you mean?'

'I mean the change in rules.' Dashy's father looked up from his plate of bacon and tomatoes. 'I mean the 'no back pass' rule. A goalkeeper is there to use his hands and now he's being told that he can't. Stupid.' He pointed at his newspaper. 'And now they're talking of making the goals bigger. Rules that have stood for decades are now no longer good enough. You might think I live in the past but if it was good enough for Moore and Charlton it should be good enough for today's players. That's all I mean.'

'You've got to move with the times,' Dashy said, and sat down with a bowl of cornflakes. It was a long time since he'd heard his father string together so many words, even if they were miserable ones. He looked across the table at him. He looked tired and lifeless. Dashy wondered how people came to terms with ageing. Did you just let it happen or was there something you could do to slow it down? Despite his father's black beard, his hair was rapidly turning grey. Dashy couldn't figure out why the beard wasn't turning grey too. Did his father dye it? Surely not. He looked at his fathers hands holding the newspaper. They were small hands, wrinkled, but almost feminine-looking; you didn't get rough hands from working in a shop. Dashy would like to have rough hands himself, the type that showed he'd done some hard labour in his lifetime.

'Are you taking on Christmas staff this year?' he asked.

His father looked surprised. 'The way things are going we'll be lucky to survive until Christmas.'

'I take it that means no.'

'If you're looking for work you shouldn't be coming to me.'

'I'm running out of alternatives.'

'You should've thought about that before you punched your foreman.'

'Thanks.'

Dashy thought back to the day he'd been sacked. He couldn't even remember why he'd hit Angus the foreman, or what they'd been arguing about. All he could remember was that Danny's face had been in his mind for the whole shift, and it had only left when he'd landed that terrific punch. It had been great to see Angus crumpled up on the warehouse floor, a look of fear in his eyes. Dashy had sensed his co-workers admiring him; they had all wanted to punch Angus for years, but he had been the first one to do it. For the first time in his life he'd actually stood out from the crowd for one frozen moment.

Dashy's job had been lorry loader, lifting heavy sacks of cat litter on to lorries for most of his eight hour day, or bagging the stuff up from silos. He hadn't minded the job, had done it for three years. After all the building work he'd done before – digging ditches, mixing concrete – it seemed a whole lot easier. Now he was twenty-five and potentially unemployable. He'd never get a reference from his last job.

'Have you got anything else lined up?' his father asked.

'There's not a lot around. But how can I apply for it anyway? They want details of all my old jobs. I give them the factory they'll find out I was sacked. They're not going to employ me. I can't lie about not working at the factory because what have I done for the last three years? It's a long gap to cover up.'

His father held up his hands. 'I haven't got an answer.'

They'd had this conversation before but now Dashy was feeling more desperate. When he'd first lost his job he'd thought about gambling as a career, and he'd had enough saved up to start doing it. Now all that money was gone – nearly five hundred pounds – and his dole money would last about a day the way his luck was going. He'd have to find something soon or else give up gambling and become a vegetable at home.

He looked at his father. 'You couldn't lend me a fiver could you?'

His father shook his head. 'You'll only lose it on a horse.'

Dashy couldn't argue with that. So much for getting up early and catching his father before he went to work. In future he'd lie in bed until he was gone.

Six

As Chris walked towards the YMCA on Friday night, he saw Amanda waiting in the foyer for him. Then he saw her car parked outside. Now that was what he called bad timing. He pushed through the swing doors and said hello to her. She stood up.

'I came to see how you were. Your face looks much better.'

'Thanks. Come along and I'll make you a coffee.' He led her down the corridor.

Inside his room, Chris put the kettle on, while Amanda sat in his only armchair. The room was warm, as it always was when he returned in the evening. The night was mild though, so he turned off the heater. He drew the curtains and leaned on the long white-topped desk that ran under the window. Amanda was looking at the room.

'Well, it's better than last time I was here. You've got a few pictures up.'

Chris nodded. The only time Amanda had been here before was two months earlier when she helped him move in, the day they'd split up for good, the day he'd rather forget about. Although Amanda had said she'd visit the previous Sunday, the day after his mugging, Chris had rung to tell her not to bother. Now she was obviously not going to wait for an invitation.

'The place needs pictures,' Chris said.

'I like the frames,' Amanda said.

Chris had bought two glass picture frames from Habitat and in the smaller one had put a glossy photo of Nastassia Kinski (he couldn't find any of Jamie Lee Curtis), and in the other a spectacular skiing shot, the shot taken at a low angle as the skier came hurtling over a hill. He'd never been skiing himself, but he liked the look of speed in the picture and the skier's flashy black racing pants and red jacket.

'They brighten the place up,' Chris said.

'Can't you paint the walls?'

'No. They have to have them all the same. You couldn't ask to paint the walls in a hotel could you.'

'They could do with it though.'

Chris turned to the kettle and started to make coffee. He didn't think the walls were that bad, even though they were light brown. He thought the carpet was worse, a sort of shit-brown colour that never looked very clean. It was just like Amanda to walk in someplace and start redecorating it in her mind. When they were living together – a rented flat down the road – she'd started redecorating their future home in her mind before they'd even decided on buying somewhere. That's when he'd started to get worried, thinking maybe it was time they split up.

He handed her a mug of instant.

'How's work?' Amanda asked.

'Okay.'

'Has your head office rung you, yet?'

'No. Why should they?'

'To thank you.'

'No.'

'You should also get some kind of compensation.'

'What for?'

'For your clothes at least. They got dirty didn't they?'

'You mean I should ask them for a cleaning bill?'

'No. Ask them to buy you new things. I would.'

Chris's trousers had been smeared with oil when he'd been mugged, and he'd thrown them away. His jacket had been stained too. It would be nice to get some replacements.

'I'll give them a ring on Monday,' he said.

'My father wants you to come to lunch on Sunday,' Amanda said. 'He's worried about your face and thinks they're not feeding you properly here.'

Chris had to smile. He was glad her old man was concerned. He hadn't even rung his own parents about the mugging yet, and wouldn't tell them until he was all healed up. He doubted if they'd show much sympathy anyway. They had retired to Wales a few years earlier and took less and less interest about what was happening in his life, or even the rest of the world. He was an only child and often wished he had a brother or sister he could talk to.

'Okay, tell him I'll be there. What sort of time?'

'Come at twelve.' He saw Amanda brightening up.

Chris sneaked a look at his watch. He was going on his first date with Liz and he needed a shower.

'Listen, I have to go and get my meal before the canteen closes,' he said.

Amanda gave him a sour look. 'I know you want to get rid of me.'

'It's not that at all. You should let me know when you're coming. The canteen closes at seven. Anyway, I'll see you on Sunday.'

'Let me at least finish my coffee.'

They talked about Amanda's job for five minutes. She worked for a travel agency in central London and enjoyed it most of the time. Chris was glad Amanda had a demanding job to take her mind off things.

When she'd finished her coffee he walked her back to the foyer. He kissed her goodbye and walked towards the canteen. Then he had to turn right, go up the stairs by the canteen entrance, and walk back to his room via the first floor. He didn't really need to reach the canteen before seven. He'd be eating out tonight with Liz.

*

Chris got to The Bulls Head pub early and sat with a pint at the bar. It was the biggest pub in Elmhurst with a large semi-circular saloon bar connected to the smaller public one, then a separate lounge with big armchairs, and a small restaurant in the back. Chris had already booked a table for later. He had asked Liz out that morning, their third conversation at the bus stop. She had seemed quite keen to come out with him so Chris would see where it led. She wouldn't be the love of his life but he'd given up on that theory since his break with Amanda. His new philosophy would be to enjoy it while he could. He wasn't in any hurry to get involved again.

Chris didn't see Liz come in, just felt a tap on his shoulder.

'Thought you'd get an early start?' she said to him.

Chris turned and smiled. 'I'm always nervous on first dates.'

'Me too.'

Liz sat on a stool next to him and Chris had a good look. He was interested to see what she'd look like out of office clothes. Thankfully most of her make-up had gone, and she was only wearing pale pink lipstick and light blue eye-shadow. Her short hair had just been washed and he wanted to run his fingers through it. She looked friendlier, less business like.

'What're you drinking?' he asked.

'A spritzer, I think.'

Chris signalled to the barman. He looked at Liz and told her she looked good.

'I put on an act for work,' she said. 'I'm afraid I believe in power dressing. The queen bitch image. I think people take notice of you more.'

Chris nodded. 'Men like their women to look efficient at work and sexy in the evening. It's a sad state of affairs.'

'You mean I don't look sexy in my suits?' she teased.

'You look sexier now.'

She was wearing a thin red leather jacket, a jumper of mixed golds and yellows, black slacks, and a pair of short length crimson leather boots. Chris had settled on black jeans for the occasion, a shiny pair of brown leather shoes, a light blue denim shirt, and his favourite jacket, brown leather with thick fur on the collar.

Chris paid for the drinks. 'I thought we'd eat here,' he said. 'They've got a nice restaurant in the back and we can stumble in here afterwards.'

'We'd better book a table then.'

'I already have.'

After one more drink they went into the dimly-lit restaurant and were shown to their table. It was a small room with a low roof and beams, and most of the other tables were occupied. The floor was polished wood and the tables had white tablecloths and napkins folded into wine glasses. There was a candle in the middle of each table, a perfect setting for romance Chris thought.

'I've never been here before,' he said as they sat down. 'Have you?'

'Two or three times.'

'On other dates?'

'With my parents usually.'

Over starters, Chris found out some more about Liz. He asked how she came to be working for a film company.

'I went to University in Nottingham,' she said, 'and came out with a degree which didn't do me any favours. Sociology. I wanted to go into publishing but ended up working in a bookshop in the West End. The pay was terrible but we used to get free tickets for films before they were released.'

'Why's that?'

Liz was eating melon while Chris had fried mushrooms. They had a half bottle of Piesporter to wash it down. Chris didn't like paying restaurant prices for wine because he could get a third off where he worked.

'Because where there's a film there's usually a book. They're called film tie-ins. The publishers would hand out free tickets so you'd go to the film, see how wonderful it was, and hopefully sell their book a little harder.'

'I'm with you. Actually, I've read a few of those. They're usually badly-written.'

'Books for people who don't read much.'

'Or who want to re-live the film.'

'Well, from going to those free previews I started meeting a few people in the film business and that's how I got my present job.'

'So what do you do during the day?'

'I type letters and make phone calls,' Liz laughed.

'Interesting.'

'But it'll lead to other things. Isn't that what everyone says?'

Chris smiled. 'So you've had two jobs. You must be pretty young.'

'I'm twenty-five.'

'That's young.'

'You can't be that much older.'

'Try eight years.'

'You don't look it.'

'I've had an easy life,' Chris said.

'So how come you're not married?'

'I'm gay.'

Liz looked at him and then smiled. 'That's what everyone thinks, I suppose.'

'If you're not hitched by my age you do get a few funny looks. Personally I think forty is about the right age to get married.'

'Have you ever been close?'

Chris told her about Amanda.

'I guess I just fell out of love with her. It happens. I've never been in love enough with anyone to want to go the whole distance with them.'

'Don't you regret that?'

'Yes and no. I don't want kids though.'

'I do. At least three!' Liz laughed. Chris couldn't think of anything worse than having three kids.

When the main course came – they were both having lamb – Chris told Liz about his varied working life.

'I left school without any exams,' he said. 'I drifted from job to job. Menial things like factory work, car park attendant, airport cleaning, that sort of stuff.'

'What's airport cleaning?'

'Cleaning out aeroplanes at Gatwick. I used to live near there. It was shift work. We'd go in and clean all the planes. Hoover them, clean the toilets, that sort of thing, ready for the next flight out. It had some good perks. You'd never believe some of the things we'd find. People would leave behind watches, bracelets, all kinds of valuables.'

'But you'd hand them in.'

'You're joking,' Chris said.

'You kept them?'

'Only the things I wanted. I always knew what time it was.'

'You're a crook.'

Chris smiled and had a sip of wine. They were on a bottle of Cotes Du Rhone now. It would cost him nearly nine pounds when the evening was over, and he knew its shelf price was nearer four. He was enjoying the food though. A bit like a Sunday lunch but who cared?

'And then you went into off-licenses?' Liz asked.

'No, you're jumping the gun. I've had fifteen jobs altogether. I won't go through them all.'

'Fifteen? Tell me some.'

'Okay. Fork lift driver, farm hand, fitting the interior of caravans. Let's see. Office cleaning, worked on a building sight once. Window cleaner. That sort of thing.'

'You should write a book.'

'They're hardly exciting enough to write about. So after doing all those for years I decided it was time to try for something a little better. I applied to work in a record shop.'

'Do you know a lot about music?'

'More than most. I grew up liking The Beatles and The Stones, graduated to Bob Dylan, that sort of thing. Nowadays I'm fairly narrow minded. I can't stand most pop music. I like Springsteen and I like a lot of country music.'

Liz pulled a face.

Chris decided to skip the reason why he'd left record retailing. Or should it be the other way around? The shop he'd worked in had been in Crawley, a busy independent store with five people working there. Chris had his own set of keys and on Sundays he would drive to the shop and steal CDs and records for his friends and their friends. He would sell them for a cheaper price than they'd be able to buy them, and he started to put the money into a separate account for future use. The shop used to write off a certain percentage of stock to pilfering anyway, so it was never detected at stock-takes. Plus their paperwork was so sloppy.

Then one Sunday Chris was caught by the manager as he walked out of the back door with five albums under his arm. The manager had left his wallet there the night before and had come to pick it up. Chris was sacked on the spot. The manager had threatened legal action but had never gone through with it. By that time Chris had managed to save nearly a thousand pounds in two years of stealing.

'I packed in record shops,' Chris continued, 'and left the Surrey, Sussex area as well. I thought if I moved elsewhere my luck would change.'

'And did it?'

'For a while. I moved to Kent, and decided to become self-employed.'

'Doing what?'

'I started up a mobile disco.'

Liz was smiling at him, but Chris was used to this reaction.

'I had a good collection of singles from the shop,' Chris said, thinking how he'd stolen most of those as well, 'so with my savings I bought the disco equipment and advertised myself as a sixties specialist. I called my disco the "60/45 Show. Swing to the Sixties with my forty-fives." I didn't want to play any disco rubbish. Things were slow to start with but they eventually picked up. I was on the dole as well.'

'It's all coming out.'

Chris wondered if he was talking too much, but what did it matter? They had finished their main course now and were waiting for dessert.

'I only had to do one or two gigs a week to survive. It was a cushy period of my life. Nearly two years.'

'And how did it end?'

'I got my equipment nicked one evening from the back of my van. I had a dark green VW to travel around in. The stuff wasn't insured and I couldn't afford to replace it. I was pretty pissed off but I got over it.'

'And went into off-licenses?'

'Yeah.'

'What made you want to do that?'

'I like drinking.'

'That's a good enough reason.'

'But now I've had enough of that too.' Chris paused and drank the last of his wine. 'I'm hoping it'll lead to other things.'

*

After an apple pie dessert they sat with coffee and bourbon. Liz had wanted Glenfiddich but Chris told her it was rubbish. He ordered Jim Beam instead. He was sipping it feeling very hazy, almost sleepy. He had to get up in the morning for work and didn't want to get too drunk, but it seemed it was too late for that now. He looked across at Liz and she was getting that sleepy look too.

'Do you want to hear something sensational?' Chris asked her. He had been wanting to tell someone since Wednesday. He hadn't told Amanda because she would just worry.

'Fire away,' Liz said.

Chris paused for effect. 'I think I've found out who mugged me.' He watched Liz sit up a bit straighter.

'You're joking,' she said. 'How did you find that out?'

'A bit of amateur sleuthing,' Chris said modestly. He told Liz about the position of the bank, the bookies, and the coffee shop in Boroughheath High Street.

'I guessed that the coffee shop would be an ideal place for someone to watch my routine from and then I thought about the bookies. Someone loses money one day, goes for a consoling cup of coffee, and sees me walking out with a bag of money. Easy pickings he thinks.'

'So you went into the coffee shop?'

'No. I went in the bookies one lunchtime just to have a look around. As I was leaving these two guys walked in and the tall dark one gave me a funny look. Actually it wasn't a funny look, it was downright scared.'

'You recognised him?'

'No. I never got a good look at him when I was mugged, but

I judged his size and general shape. That guy fitted it perfectly. He was also wearing a ring on his right hand. It was a ring that made this mark on my cheek. It gave me the shivers. I'm sure it was him.'

'So what are you going to do about it?'

'I don't know.'

'Tell the police.'

'I don't think they can do anything about it. I suppose they could bring the chap in for questioning, but he could just deny it all. I've got no solid proof. He's sure to have worked out an alibi by now.'

'Why don't you have a talk with that policeman you saw?'

'That's probably the best thing. Trouble is, I can't remember his name. He could be from anywhere.'

'Ask in the police station. Describe him to them.'

'Yeah.'

Chris finished his bourbon. It was time to think about paying. Liz was giving him a funny look.

'You're not going to do anything silly about this are you?'

'Like what?' Chris asked innocently.

'Become a vigilante?'

'No,' Chris laughed. 'I wouldn't dream of it.'

After Chris had paid the bill with his Visa card they went into the bar for a final drink. Then they left. They walked arm in arm through Elmhurst and looked in the windows of antique shops. Some of the shops already had Christmas displays in their windows. It was a mild night, almost as mild as a summers evening.

'I wonder if anyone actually buys anything in these shops,' Chris said.

'They don't need to,' Liz said.

'Why?'

'Because the husband works in London. Usually he has his own business. He buys an antique shop for his wife to work in during the day and writes it off against tax. I should know because this shop here is ours.'

They were standing in front of an antique shop which had tastefully arranged nightlights in the window. The shop looked a comfortable place, like someone's sitting-room, except it was filled with too much furniture.

'Your family owns this?' Chris asked.

Liz nodded. 'My mother sits in here all day dressed to the hilt. I often wonder what she does with herself.'

'It's not busy, I take it.'

'No. An average of three customers a day I should think. As long as they don't expect me to take it over.'

They walked down the main road past the YMCA, then turned right down the road to Liz's house. After a few minutes they came to a house with an inward curving white wall at the front, the driveway going through the centre. Beyond that there was a circular driveway with a round patch of lawn in the middle. On the lawn was a single lamp to light the area. There were two big cars parked in front of the large white house. Chris looked at the sign on the white wall. It said *The White House*. He was going to make some crack about American politics but decided against it. Probably everyone said that to Liz. Instead he just said, 'Nice.'

'Would you like to come in for coffee?' Liz asked.

'We just had one.'

'So have another.'

'Are your parents in?' Chris could see a light on downstairs.

'Yes.'

'I'll give it a miss then. I have to be up early anyway.'

'Okay. Give me a kiss goodnight.'

Chris put his hands on Liz's waist and pulled her towards him. It felt unusual kissing someone who wasn't Amanda, but it was something he'd have to get used to. He kissed her again to get more practice.

'I'll see you on Monday,' he said. 'I'll be the one waiting for a bus.'

'Okay.'

'I can't make it tomorrow night and Sunday I'm going out.' Why was he making excuses already?

'That's all right. I'm not in any hurry.'

Chris smiled. He wanted to tell Liz that another serious relationship was the last thing he needed. He still needed some breathing space after Amanda. He could tell her that next time though.

'I'll see you Monday,' he said again, then walked back to the YMCA.

Seven

'You never thought about this place, did you?' Kevin said.

Dashy shook his head.

They were standing in the car park on top of the Boroughheath Shopping Mall. There were two levels of parking with open sides all the way around. It meant you could stand and look down at the street below. Especially the High Street.

'You must've had your eyes closed,' Kevin said. 'Sitting in the coffee shop down there, all you had to do was look up.'

That's what Kevin had done yesterday evening. They'd walked out of the bookies and Kevin had stood there loosening his neck, turning his head around to get rid of the stiffness. His head had been pointing upwards and he'd seen the car park, rising opposite, suddenly getting ideas. He wasn't going to tell Dashy it was a fluke. They were looking down on the High Street now, hiding themselves from the parking area behind a cement pillar. Behind them people were parking cars and pushing trolleys full of groceries. Below them they could see the traffic, the bookies, the bank, and the side road. They were watching people going to the nightsafe. Banking Saturday's takings.

'Do you recognise any of these people?' Kevin asked.

'Most of them.'

'Tell me about them. Here comes one now.'

They watched as a man walked along the side street away from them, up to the nightsafe, unlocked it and shoved in his money.

'He's from the Reject Shop,' Dashy said. 'The manager I think. I didn't like the look of him. Looks a tough little bastard.'

'You think the off-licence bloke looked a pushover?'

'No. He looked like he had brains. I thought he'd be the type to let me do it. I didn't think he'd risk going for me.'

Kevin nodded. 'What about all these girls coming out. Did you think about them?'

'They would be the easiest but I didn't want to do them.'

'Why not?'

'Because they're girls.'

Kevin was surprised at the amount of teenagers carrying their shop's takings; in carrier bags with the shop's name emblazoned on them in bright colours. Why did their managers let them do it? It was inviting trouble. He watched the three young girls, each with dyed hair frizzed up, wearing modern clothes, laughing and joking as they walked, not taking any care at all, carrying all that money. They even had trouble with the nightsafe, pulling on the handle with nothing happening. Two of them had to almost swing on it, laughing all the time. Meanwhile the carrier bag was hanging there loosely, waiting to be scooped up.

'Where do they work?' Kevin asked.

'One of those clothes shops. You can tell by the way they dress.'

'Did you make a list of all these people? Work out who would be the most profitable?'

Dashy shook his head. 'I just knew them by sight. I didn't take notes. I reckoned whatever any of them had would be more than I had. What's the difference, a few hundred pounds here and there?'

'It may be a few thousand. It may be worth looking into.'

'Well, how would you do that?'

'Walk around the shops, look in the tills when people're being served. See if there's a lot of cash in there.'

'I didn't think of that.'

'An off-licence probably wasn't a bad choice. Lots of cash sales. A more expensive line of business though like clothes or shoes or jewellery, and the average sale must be a lot higher than beer or wine.'

'They might use credit cards more though.'

'Maybe. But a lot of people around here pay in cash. Working men with rolls of money in their pocket.'

'I should've thought all this out before. I'm glad you're along for this one.'

Kevin looked at Dashy. 'I haven't said I'll do anything yet. I'm just looking it over.'

'So look it over, here comes another one. This is a shoe shop.'

Kevin looked down again. This was interesting.

Yesterday evening after he'd stretched his neck, asked Dashy if he'd noticed the car park, Kevin had agreed to go for a drink with him for the first time. Dashy had been moping all day and looked in need of cheering up. They'd walked down the street to a pub further away, in case that off-licence man came snooping again. He'd been into the bookies three days in a row, every lunchtime since Wednesday. Dashy had been getting more nervous every time.

'I'm sure he's on to me,' Dashy had said in the pub, shaking his head, looking down into his beer.

'I think he is too,' Kevin had said.

'Thanks.'

Dashy had then told him about Helen, the greaser-looking girl, and how he'd wanted the money so he could take her out. Also about his savings, how he'd whittled them away on betting, and how he was up shit-street financially.

'Wouldn't you be tempted to steal if you were in my position?' Dashy had asked.

Kevin had thought about that before answering yes. If he was desperate enough he would.

'Are you desperate enough?' Dashy had asked.

'You mean you want to do it again?'

'If at first you don't succeed…'

'You must be mad.'

Now he was mad enough to be standing up here with Dashy, looking down on defenceless young girls, trying to pick one to knock over. He hadn't agreed to do anything yet, but why was he even thinking about it? There were two reasons…

Firstly, he had to admit he was tired of having no money, of being on the dole, of having to live frugally all the time. It would be nice to get a bundle of money, place a few decent bets and increase it to something worth having. He knew he was a good enough gambler to do that.

And secondly, he was still smarting from losing his licence and getting heavily fined for one stupid little night of drinking. He'd read in the paper only that morning of a hit and run driver who'd been fined less than he had! The whole legal system was out of proportion. He felt someone owed him something for the year he was losing out on good driving wages. Someone had to pay him back.

'Here're a couple of girls,' Dashy was saying. 'I thought they'd be easy. It's the same two almost every night.'

'A couple of lookers.'

'Pity we couldn't share it with them,' Dashy laughed.

'You'd have less money for yourself.'

'Kidnap them. Have our way with them and leave them.'

Kevin ignored that one. 'The thing here is to have more than one choice. You could bide your time then. If the situation didn't look right, you could wait for the next group. Did you have someone in reserve if the off-licence man didn't come out?'

'No. It was him or nothing.'

Kevin could see why Dashy's mugging hadn't worked. He'd left most of it to chance. Almost a spur of the moment thing. But maybe that wasn't such a bad way either. Take everyone, including yourself, by surprise. You wouldn't have to shit yourself beforehand then.

'Here he comes now,' Dashy said.

Kevin saw the guy from the off-licence walking to the night-safe, but this time he had that young girl assistant with him. He watched with interest as they put the money in. He tried to imagine the scene a week ago when Dashy had walked up and tried his luck. He pictured the struggle in the street, then Dashy running behind the bank and over the wall. He couldn't see the wall from here but he knew what it looked like. If he was going to try this on he'd make sure there was something by the wall to jump on to and help him over that height. He looked at Dashy. Poor bloke must be going through it all again as well.

'You know you were lucky,' Kevin said. 'He's not the sort of bloke I'd pick on to mug. He looks as though he can handle himself.'

'I didn't want girls. I've just told you.'

'Look at them! They're holding hands now! What a smoothy. Walk to the nightsafe and pick up the shop assistant on the way back.'

'Maybe he's going out with her.'

'You could be right.'

They watched them walk to the High Street, cross, and then disappear from sight underneath them.

Dashy looked at his watch. 'There's a few more to come yet. You get the last about six.'

'Let's watch them all. Then we'll go for a drink.'

*

Chris didn't know what was happening when Rachel grabbed his hand. He looked down at her and there she was smiling up at him.

'Don't think about it,' she said.

He smiled at her. He presumed she was talking about last Saturday. He wasn't thinking about it. He was thinking about her little hand in his. He'd already taken the money three nights in a row. Ron had said it's like falling off a horse, you've got to get back up and do it again. He'd like to know why Ron never took the money.

'I'm used to it now,' Chris said. Rachel started to take her hand away. 'But we can still hold hands.' He grabbed it back.

They walked along in silence until they came to the curb. 'Your face looks almost normal now,' Rachel said.

'It's still a bit stiff here,' Chris said, running a finger across his left cheekbone. He was finding it hard to concentrate. Was his voice shaking? Holding Rachel's hand was turning him on.

Rachel was looking at his cheek in the streetlight. 'You've still got a lump there. It looks kind of sexy though.'

'Looks pretty macho, eh?'

'It does. It looks as though you've been around.'

'A man of the world.' He was grinning now, but it hurt his cheek so he stopped. They walked across the road, bright shop windows in the early evening. As they neared the off-licence Rachel took her hand away.

'Better not let Ron see us,' she said.

'What are you doing tonight?' Chris asked. It came out before he had time to think. He heard Rachel say, 'Nothing', and caught the eagerness in her voice.

'How about coming out with me? Have a few drinks.' He felt uneasy asking and knew he shouldn't. He'd been out with Liz the previous night and was still feeling hungover, but he was in a good mood and wanted something to do. Hadn't Rachel prompted it anyway by reaching for his hand? It would be interesting. See if they could sit with each other and talk for a few hours instead of a few minutes at the till or in the staffroom.

'Okay,' Rachel said.

It was done.

*

Rachel couldn't believe she was on a date with Chris. They were in The Angel, a short walk from the off-licence and away from the Mall. The place was filling up as shop workers began their weekend, drinking away the memories of unpleasant customers. Rachel and Chris had had three drinks, talked mainly about work, both of them moaning about Ron. Rachel didn't mind talking about work. It was a good way of loosening up for other subjects. Now she watched Chris coming back from the Gents, smiling as he neared, sitting down next to her, lifting up his pint.

'What are you smiling at?' she asked.

'I was thinking of a theory I came up with today. Do you want to hear it?'

'What is it?'

'It's the "Sex for a man is like losing a penalty shoot-out" theory.'

'Oh, yes?'

'It goes like this. You know how a man after he's had his orgasm just rolls off the woman and goes to sleep, or if he doesn't go to sleep, he's very remote, or let down?'

'Yes.'

'Well, it's because for him, sex is like a penalty shoot-out.'

'This I have to hear.'

'Right. Well, sex for a woman is usually on one level because usually it doesn't end with them having an orgasm.'

'Maybe you've been doing the wrong things.'

'I'll let that remark slip by unnoticed. Sex for a woman is the equivalent of a man having sex without an orgasm. Can you imagine a man withdrawing with his hard-on before orgasm and saying, "That's it, I don't want anymore"?'

Rachel laughed. 'No, I can't. A man must have his orgasm!'

'That's right. So while the man is having sex it's exciting, like he's in a penalty shoot-out. He doesn't know how it's going to end because he doesn't know if he'll have a great orgasm, an average one, or a downright disappointing one. And then after the orgasm, the feeling is one of let-down, depression, like when you miss a penalty in the shoot-out and the game is over.'

'But why does he feel depressed?'

'It's because he's gone from the high of the sex and the orgasm, to the low of it being finished a few seconds later. He's gone from high excitement to nothing in a short space of time, an experience level the woman doesn't go through. The level between the two is too much for him and therefore he can only feel let-down or depressed afterwards. I know I always do.

Maybe I expect too much. But it's usually an anti-climax, not a climax. The man always expects more, so he's disappointed. He rolls over and goes to sleep. He's lost the penalty shoot-out.'

Rachel stared at her Bacardi and coke and felt bemused. 'Well, it's an interesting theory. I'll have to think it over.'

'Take your time.'

Rachel felt easy talking about sex with Chris. Somehow, because he was older, it didn't seem as embarrassing. She'd told him some pretty personal things since she'd been working at The Wine Seller. She wasn't surprised to hear him talk so openly about orgasms.

'Remember that time I told you about Brian?' she asked him now.

'Told me what about Brian?'

'We were on the till one Saturday and I told you that I'd worn him out the night before.'

Chris smiled. 'I remember.'

'I was thinking afterwards, maybe I shouldn't have told you. But then I thought, it's too late now.'

'I was a bit shocked.'

'But it's easy telling you. I don't know why I did it.'

'I think you wanted to let me know you were grown up, that you were having regular sex.'

'You're probably right.'

'It had the added effect of turning me on too,' he teased.

'That could be another reason why I did it.'

'Was it you who ended it with him?'

'Yes. He was getting on my nerves. He talked too much. Boys go on about girls nattering away but boys do it too you know. Brian loved to talk about himself and cars. When he got on to cars I just stopped listening.'

'How long did you go out with him?'

'Six months.'

'Was he your first boyfriend?'

'My second. The first I slept with though.' There she was telling him more secrets.

'You see, I was right. You wanted to let me know you'd discovered sex. To show me you were grown up. It's a natural reaction. Normally you'd want to tell your parents, shock them a bit, but you told me instead. Maybe you think I'm as old as them!'

'I didn't mean it like that!' They both laughed.

'Have you ever thought about us going out together?' Rachel asked. She'd had three Bacardi and cokes and now was the time to get on to something interesting, find out a few secrets. Chris was nodding.

'Many times. I've always fancied you. I've always thought I was too old though. We could go out and it would last only a few months.'

'It might be fun though.' Was she pushing too hard? She could see him feeling uncomfortable. Maybe she should back off.

'We'd have to work with each other afterwards. Have you ever thought of that?'

Rachel shook her head. 'I'm not there every day anyway.'

Now he was looking distracted. He was looking into the other bar, straining his neck. Damn! She had pushed it too far. Now he was standing up.

'Hang on. I'm just going into the other bar a second.'

Rachel watched him push through the crowd again and head towards the Gents. Did he need to go again already? She felt uncomfortable sitting on her own. Other men were looking at her, trying to catch her eye. The male population in general drove her up the wall the way they fancied themselves: workmen giving her wolf-whistles on the street, louts trying to chat her up on trains, and now drunkards eyeing her in the pub. She wished Chris would hurry back so they could get back to their conversation. It was just getting interesting. Then she saw him in the other bar. He had been to the toilet again. Maybe he'd gone to buy some condoms. Maybe tonight it was going to happen! But surely it was too soon. This time as he came towards her he wasn't smiling at all. He had a stern look on his face and she felt scared of him. He didn't sit down either, just reached for his pint and finished it standing up.

'Let's go,' he said to her.

Rachel finished her drink and followed him out, thinking, what did I do wrong?

*

Chris led Rachel away from the pub and into another fifty yards away. It was small and cramped and they had to push their way through to the bar. They stood squashed against each other waiting for their drinks.

'Why the sudden departure?' Rachel asked him. Or shouted. It was loud in there, with a jukebox blaring and people raising their voices to make themselves heard.

'I saw someone I wanted to avoid,' Chris said.

'That's a relief. I thought it was me.'

Chris smiled at her, glad he was out of The Angel.

'Let's move away from here,' he said.

They took their drinks and moved from the bar. There was nowhere to sit, so they stood uncomfortably in the middle of the room, people pushing by them to get through for drinks. Chris started to feel uneasy and old. Here he was with a seventeen year old on a Saturday night standing in a pub full of other youngsters; youngsters making a row, dressed in trendy clothes, laughing too loudly, showing everyone what a great time they were having. He didn't think he could stand more than one drink. He looked down at Rachel next to him. He could see she was uneasy too.

'Well, here we are,' he said.

Rachel smiled. Chris felt like kissing her but that could come later when they said goodnight. But would a kiss mean he was committing himself? He still wasn't sure what was going on or what he was doing. Last night he'd been out with Liz and kissed her goodnight. Now here he was with Rachel, and he could get another kiss tonight as well. Then what would he do? Go home and decide between the two? Pick the one with the best kiss? He had to admit it wasn't a bad position to be in, but was another girlfriend what he needed right now?

'How about we do this sometime during the week?' Chris said. 'I don't like Saturday night crowds.'

'Will you walk me to the bus stop? I don't like it in the dark.'

'Sure.'

When they got out of there Chris took hold of Rachel's hand. He liked the feel of it in his, liked the size of her next to him. He was thinking about the goodnight kiss to come, hoping there wouldn't be too many people at the bus stop watching. They made small talk as they walked, Chris starting to feel nervous and sensing that Rachel was too.

When they got to the bus stop there were five other people there. Chris cursed his luck and led Rachel behind the iron shelter. Now they couldn't be seen by anyone.

'That was crafty,' Rachel said.

Chris took her in his arms. He'd been wanting to try this for months. He bent down and they kissed, Rachel pushing a bit too eagerly, forcing her tongue a bit too much. He broke the kiss and told her not to push so hard. The next kiss was better, softer, but Rachel's body was pushing hard getting him aroused. She certainly didn't hold back.

'I hear a bus,' Chris said.

'Shall I catch the next one?' Rachel asked.

Chris shook his head. 'I'll see you Monday.'

He remembered telling that to Liz too.

Eight

After Rachel's bus had pulled away, Chris headed back towards The Angel. It was nearly ten o'clock and he hoped he wasn't too late. On the way, he stopped briefly at The Wine Seller and pinched a quarter bottle of whisky. He had pinched bottles before and was long past the feeling guilty stage. Even his getting caught at the record shop hadn't put him off stealing from his employers. He knew it was something most people did one way or the other, people just differed in how often they did it, that's all.

When he got to The Angel he walked around the saloon bar. He squeezed through people, trying not to knock drinks out of their hands. That would be a good one; start an argument with someone while he was trying to go unnoticed. He eventually made it to the public bar, poked his head between two girls, and saw his curly headed mugger still sitting there with a beer. He pushed his way back to the street.

He crossed the main road looking for somewhere to hide. There was a garage with new cars on the forecourt, price stickers on their windscreens. He stepped over a chain at the entrance and crouched behind a brand new Rover, giving himself a good view of the front door of the pub. He took out his whisky and had a nip. He could be in for a long wait.

Chris thought of Rachel. He'd have to make it up to her for his strange behaviour. He'd been enjoying the evening until he'd seen his mugger and that blonde friend of his. He'd been a bit wary, going round to the Gents again, making sure it was really them, and then letting himself be seen just to get them on edge. But if he kept on annoying them with his presence, then something would have to give eventually.

As for Rachel, he'd effectively ended the evening by marching her out of the pub, but she seemed keen on him and the goodnight kiss had made up for it. He relived it again, comparing it to Liz's kiss. Rachel won on points. Not for proficiency, but for excitement. He took another sip of whisky then remembered he had to be at Amanda's tomorrow for Sunday lunch. With all that had happened in the last two days he didn't feel like going at all. He'd be hungover too. Still, he couldn't get out of it now.

An hour later people started leaving the pub. Chris was cold and stiff from crouching, and was wishing he could run up and down the street a few times. Then he saw his mugger coming out of the pub followed by the blonde chap. They turned to their right and started walking down the street. Chris stood up, glad to be on the move, and stiffly followed them from his side of the street.

They walked slowly for about ten minutes, past the Shopping Mall, down to the unfashionable end of Boroughheath. Chris could hear their laughter, and Curly's loud voice. The more he saw them, the more he disliked them.

They walked past where the new superstore was being built, an octagonal building of black glass with a vertical yellow and green sign that said, *Asda*. Chris had never seen anything so ugly. Residents had been complaining about it since day one. Chris thought it looked about as welcoming as an abattoir. Then they passed the LEB building, a massive office block with a showroom to the side that was about half the size of a football pitch, full of washing machines and fridges.

Chris thought they were heading for Shooters Hill until Blondie waved goodbye and began to cross over to Chris's side of the street. Then he started walking back towards Chris! Chris quickly crossed to Curly's side, keeping his head down.

Chris was now between the two of them and thought for a moment that maybe he'd just walked into a trap. Then he was passing Blondie, both of them on opposite sides of the street going in different directions. Chris looked up and noticed that Curly had disappeared! He was starting to get worried. Curly could be waiting for him up ahead, with Blondie turning and closing in from behind. He started to wish he'd gone straight home. The last thing he needed was another swollen face. But then he thought, if they did beat him up, that would be like admitting their guilt. He started to relax.

At the next turning, Avenue Road, Chris looked right and saw Curly still walking. He felt relieved and turned after him. They walked for a couple of hundred yards, before Curly opened a gate and headed for a house. Chris had to start jogging, then sprinting, so he could see exactly which house Curly had gone into. He got there just in time, seeing the front door close, the rectangle of light disappearing. He looked at the number of the house. Seventeen. That would be easy to remember. Rachel's age. He turned and started the long walk back to the High Street. He hoped he could still get a bus home at that time of night.

*

Kevin dodged into someone's front garden as he saw Mr Off-Licence coming back up the street. He hid behind a sorry-looking tree, the only piece of foliage in a garden full of paving stones. It was just thick enough to hide him. There was a light on in the sitting-room behind him and he could hear the TV. Next he heard footsteps as Offie walked by, still catching his breath after chasing Dashy.

Kevin waited a minute then followed. So what was Offie up to?

He couldn't believe it when he'd seen him on the other side of the street a few minutes earlier, walking with his head down as if that would stop him from being noticed. Kevin had thought about it for a second, then crossed over and followed. Maybe the guy was going to jump Dashy. Kevin had been worried when he'd seen the running, had started to run too. But Dashy had disappeared into Helen's house. Now why would Offie follow Dashy to Helen's house and then leave it at that? Kevin thought about it a minute and then started to smile. Because he thought that was where Dashy lived! He thought he was being smart following Dashy home, thought that maybe that bit of information might come in useful some day. There was Offie walking up the street ahead of him feeling pretty pleased with himself. See Dashy in the pub by fluke, follow him home, maybe give his address to the police and get them to question him.

Kevin almost started laughing. It was a bit of luck Dashy hadn't gone straight home. He'd been feeling depressed in the pub, even before Offie had made an appearance. Then he'd sunk even lower and had decided to visit Helen's to try and cheer himself up. A good job he had.

Now Mr Off-Licence was jogging up the street away from him. What was he trying to do, keep fit? Kevin crossed the road and got back on the route he'd been taking five minutes earlier.

*

Chris had got home at ten minutes past midnight, the magical hour when the YMCA lock their front door. He'd had to stand outside in the cold for ten minutes until the security guard had returned from the toilet or wherever he'd been. Then he'd knocked on the glass door and the old boy hadn't even heard him. He'd walked right past with his personal stereo on, through a door and into his little office. Chris thought old people looked ridiculous with those things on. Most young people did too. Chris could see him through the serving hatch, settling down for the night, turning on his portable TV. He couldn't believe it. He'd started banging on the door then and the old boy had looked up…

Fourteen hours later, Chris was on Amanda's front doorstep, banging on her door.

'We'd given up on you,' she said, when she answered.

'I didn't think it was so far away,' Chris replied, complaint being the last thing he needed after a half hour walk. He was sweating underneath his coat and still felt hungover.

'I could've given you a lift if you'd rung,' Amanda said.

'Now she tells me.'

They went into the sitting-room and Chris peeled off his coat. He'd been to Amanda's father's house before of course, but this was the first time since they'd split up. Her father came in from the kitchen, drying his hands on a towel.

'Afternoon, Chris,' he said. He reached out a dried hand and they shook.

'Hello Jim,' Chris said. He always felt uncomfortable calling Amanda's father by his first name but that's what Jim liked. Chris was pleased to see him. Every time he saw Jim he looked a little heavier. He'd been retired about six months from a warehouse job. Before that he'd spent the best part of his life on the docks, a stevedore with arms of steel. He still looked strong, despite the extra weight. He might have a heart attack if he swung at you, but the punch would be sure to lay you out.

'Been out in the garden,' Jim said.

'You're always out in the garden,' Chris smiled. 'I think you only do it for the tan.'

'Not in this weather I don't.'

'You're looking well, anyway.' Chris liked the way Jim looked. He'd be pleased if he looked as good at that age. Jim was bald down the middle of his head and his white hair was cut short. His face and forearms were a deep brown. Chris would like to pull the hairs out of Jim's nose sometime, but he supposed at that age there were few women you had to impress. Amanda's mother had died six years earlier and Jim had been alone ever since.

'And you're not looking too bad either,' Jim said. 'All things considered.'

'You should see the other bloke,' Chris joked.

'You've still got a lump there though.'

'Lumps go away. A few months and nothing'll notice.'

Jim nodded. 'How about a drink? Beer, sherry?'

Jim poured three sherries as Chris sank down into the sofa, Amanda beside him. It was a comfortable room, sofa and armchairs with plenty of cushions, a standard lamp, an old colour TV, and a polished wooden cabinet-style record player. You didn't see many of those around any more. There were scenic paintings on the walls, the type that stay up for years, that no one really looks at or questions why they're there. Chris preferred his picture of Nastassia Kinski.

'Three o'clock it starts,' Jim was saying. 'Who do you think'll win?'

'Palace, hopefully,' Chris said. It looked as though there was live football on TV that afternoon. Amanda started to groan.

*

Amanda was picking at some grapes wishing she'd bought the seedless type. She was having to take them out of her mouth with her fingers, and it wasn't the prettiest sight for Chris opposite. Lining them up on her plate. Well, he'd seen worse before, knew more intimate things about her than that. She liked having him there, although she knew he'd be gone in a few hours and when would she see him again after that?

Getting to see him was like trying to see Prince Charles. He was getting more and more distant and eventually he'd disappear. He seemed to enjoy his new found freedom and days like these were just minor interruptions in his new life. Well, stuff him.

'That sort of thing,' her father was saying. 'It's the sort of thing you think will never happen to you.'

Chris popped a grape into his mouth. 'It's always someone else. Now I know that's not true.'

Here we go, Amanda thought. A discussion on the mugging again. She caught Chris's eye.

Her father said: 'I don't know what's going on these days, I swear I don't. Every day there seems to be something on the news. People getting attacked, children going missing. That's the worse thing. I'd like to get my hands on some of them. Show them a thing or two.'

'You'd run the other way,' Amanda laughed.

'I wouldn't. If I knew someone who was assaulting a kid I'd have them. And no second thoughts.'

'They get it when they go to prison, anyway,' Amanda said. 'Other criminals don't like that type.'

'That's no compensation for parents. But it's better than nothing. Personally I'd shoot them all.'

Amanda looked at Chris smiling. 'Have you told your parents yet?'

Chris shook his head. She saw that look come into his eyes whenever the parents subject came up. A hardness and a narrowing. 'There's no point. They wouldn't worry about it and I'd only have to go through the whole story again.'

Sometimes she hated him. Why did he have to act so cold towards his family? She'd only met them once, the previous Christmas when she'd finally persuaded him that he owed them a visit. What a terrible two days that had been. Chris had hardly spoken to his father at all, and his mother hardly said two words. Mostly it was his father holding forth, telling long boring stories about neighbours and friends Amanda knew nothing about.

Chris's father fancied himself as a cook and always did the honours at Christmas, but took half a day to prepare the meals. They'd be sitting in front of the television, Chris and his mother drinking continually without getting drunk, until finally the call to the table came. By then it would be three or four hours later than normal people ate. Amanda had been glad to get out of the house after that experience, and the first thing Chris had said, as soon as his parents had dropped them at the station was, Didn't I tell you? She could've hit him. She could understand why he didn't like going to visit them, but at least he could try. You didn't get anything without trying.

Now her father was getting up, carrying dishes to the sink.

'Leave them, Dad. I'll do them later,' Amanda said.

'I'll get them out of the way.'

'I'll give you a hand,' Chris said, without moving from his seat.

'You're the guest,' her father said.

Chris smiled at Amanda. They'd often joked in the past about her father's need to wash up immediately a meal was finished. He couldn't relax or sit still, unless it was to watch football or snooker.

'Would you like to see my room?' Amanda asked Chris.

'Okay,' he said, a guilty look coming on to his face.

She led him upstairs and into the spare bedroom which had been her home for the last two months. When they'd moved her stuff in on that terrible day, they'd just dumped it all on the floor and Chris had said, You'll never get all that in here. Well, now she wanted to show him that she had, that he wasn't the only person in the world who could survive on his own.

'It looks good,' he said as they entered. Standing there nodding his head, looking impressed.

'I'm using this foldaway bed,' Amanda said, 'but it's okay. I've put blankets underneath to give it more padding.' She opened the wardrobe and showed Chris. 'I've got everything in here.' He was nodding again, taking interest but really miles away.

'You've done very well,' he said.

It didn't seem right to Amanda, Chris living in that horrible YMCA, her living in this cramped room. They could be somewhere together, living so much more comfortably. She watched him step to the window and look down at the garden below. Something was on his mind. Now he was turning around.

'Can I ask your opinion on something?' he asked her.

'You're going to anyway.'

'Let's sit down.'

They sat on the bed together. Amanda picked up her two home-made bears and sat them on her lap.

'I know who my mugger is,' Chris said. He was leaning forward, gesturing with his hands. 'I found him when I went back to work. I saw him in the bookies one lunchtime by chance, because that's where I figured he'd hang out. I've been keeping an eye on him ever since. He hangs around a lot with a blonde friend of his.'

Amanda tried to show interest. 'You're sure it's him? I thought you didn't get a good look.'

'I know it's him. I can feel it. Plus, they act awkward whenever I'm around.'

'So?'

'So last night I saw them in the pub and followed them home. That is I followed the mugger home. They split up on the way.'

Amanda couldn't believe she was hearing this. What was Chris up to? And who had he been in the pub with? Was he dating someone already?

'So now I know where he lives, what do I do about it? Shall I go back to the cops and tell them? I don't know the muggers name, just the address, so I don't know how they'd handle it.'

Amanda looked at the window and then back at Chris. 'Go to the police. Tell them and then forget about it.'

'Let them deal with it?'

'Well what else can you do?'

'I don't know.'

Now he was annoying her. Sitting there in her new room oblivious to all the feelings going through her, worrying about his damned mugging as if it were the crime of the century. Okay, so it was an unpleasant experience but why couldn't he just forget about it? Why did he have to worry it into the ground all the time? Was he trying to prove how tough he was?

'Let's go downstairs,' she said. 'I'm sure the football's started by now.' She put the bears back on the pillow and walked out.

*

Chris got a lift home in the early evening. The three of them had watched the football, Chris and Jim knocking back a few beers. Chris had nearly fallen asleep, the drinking catching up with him. He'd have to lay off the stuff for a couple of days. Not an easy thing to do when you work in an off-licence. Chris was also regretting telling Amanda about his mugger. There he was on Friday night telling Liz about it, thinking how he wasn't going to tell Amanda because she'd only worry, and now on Sunday he'd gone and told her as well. He was telling too many people. What did he expect from them? A medal? Recognition?

Amanda was silent as she drove.

'That was a good meal,' Chris said. 'If they had a cook as good as you at the YMCA I'd stay forever.'

'You probably will anyway,' Amanda said. 'Haven't you thought of moving out yet?'

'No. I don't need to.'

'Well, don't get entrenched there.'

Chris didn't intend to. He felt he was on the verge of moving, of something about to happen so he could move out. He didn't know exactly what that was, whether it was Rachel or Liz or the mugging, but he'd had an interesting few days and he wanted to follow it through. See what became of it all.

Amanda dropped him at the front door again, just like on the night he'd been mugged. Chris kissed her goodbye and got out.

As he walked to his room Chris started feeling depressed. He opened the door, turned on the lights, and drew the curtains. He slumped into his armchair and sat looking at the wall. Although he was enjoying his new single life and the fun of going out with Rachel and Liz, this room was not the place to be on a Sunday night. He got up and went to the sink in the corner. He turned on the cold water and splashed it over his face. He dried himself and then slotted Townes Van Zandt into the cassette-radio. He turned it up as Townes started to sing *Pancho And Lefty*. Then he sat back in the armchair and looked through the newspaper to see if there was anything decent on TV. Was there ever anything decent on TV? He put the paper on the floor, got up, and lay down on his bed. In five minutes he was fast asleep.

Nine

Eunice Thomas made sure she bent over a long time. Arrange those mixers nicely, wipe the shelf, give Kevin a good look at her backside as he sat there at the bar. She straightened up quickly, saw that he'd been looking, and smiled to herself as she walked into the public bar. That should give him something to think about.

Eunice enjoyed her work at the pub, had always enjoyed working in pubs. She had only been at The Coach and Horses a few weeks, but before that had worked every evening in The Bricklayers Arms in Welling. Needing extra work she had left The Bricklayers for The C & H where she worked Monday to Friday, afternoon and evening, while still working weekends at The Bricklayers Arms. That was a seven day week but she didn't mind. What else did she have to do?

Since her husband Michael had left her, pub work was the only way Eunice knew of meeting new men. And it was a good way, too. She could get to know them slowly, pick out the one's she liked, smile at them, talk to them, and usually they'd ask her out. It depended on how she felt at the time how far she went, but she certainly wasn't ready to get involved again – it was all just a bit of fun.

In the five years since Michael had left for his life of chastity and sport, Eunice had slept with six men, plus several more gropings in cars. The gropings had been with businessmen, thank you kisses for taking her out for a good meal, sometimes letting them feel a breast, but usually no further. The business types had the money to entertain her but were usually over-weight slobs who turned her off. She was proud of her slim body, exceptional for a fifty year old, and if she could use it to attract younger men, then she was going to for as long as she could. There was plenty of time for growing old.

Eunice pulled a pint for a young man she'd never seen in the pub before. Business suit but young too. Maybe she'd go after him when she'd finished with Kevin Smarty Pants. The man, more of a boy really – weren't all men? – was watching her, so she took hold of the pump with her long fingers and nails and handled it suggestively. The young mans eyes nearly popped out of his head! She smiled at him. She loved these young ones. So much energy! Inexperienced yes, but she could always teach them things. She put down the young man's pint and went back to see Kevin.

'Miss me?' she asked, giving him a wink.

'Always miss you,' Kevin said.

Eunice leaned on the bar in front of him. The lunchtime rush hadn't started yet.

'I didn't know you cared,' she said. She could almost see him thinking, trying to use that brain of his, thinking should he try his luck?

'What do you do in the afternoons?' he asked her.

'I go home and sit around bored,' Eunice said. 'Maybe do some housework. Watch TV.'

Now he was nodding at her. Here it comes. He was leaning forward as if about to part with a great secret.

'How about letting me come home with you? We could get some wine, some Chinese food, have a little party. Better than being on your own.'

'What about your horses?'

'I'll have a day off. I'm not on a lucky streak anyway.'

'Let me think about it. I'll tell you later.'

Eunice thought that was a good touch. It was never a good thing to accept straight away, unless she really fancied them. She quite fancied Kevin, but knew it was nothing more than a physical attraction. He was quite muscular-looking in an over-the-top macho way, especially with those tattoos on his arms. She'd been flirting with him since she'd started there, and who else was there to go out with at the moment? No one. She was going through a lean spell. She hadn't slept with anyone for five months, and Kevin really fancied himself. She wanted to take him home, teach him a few tricks, show him that she knew a lot more than he ever would, and then ditch him. It would be a good start to the week. Then she could work on that young man she'd just seen. There he was again. Sitting alone with his pint.

*

Four hours later Kevin was sitting in Eunice's flat wondering when it was all going to happen. He'd been sitting in Eunice's flat for three hours now, drinking and smoking, a pile of empty Chinese takeaway cartons on the table in front of him.

He was feeling horny, but too much more to drink and he'd be reaching the stage where he couldn't get it up. It had happened before. What was Eunice doing, leading him on? And where was she now? She'd been out of the room for five minutes.

Kevin had to laugh at how easy Eunice had been, agreeing to take him home after only one time of asking. He wished all women were that easy.

They'd driven back to Eunice's flat in Welling in her Ford Cortina, a light blue machine that had seen better days. Eunice's flat was in a small block with garages in the driveway below. She had parked the car in the garage and then they'd walked up to the second floor.

The flat was a nice size for one person, the kind of place Kevin could do with. He was envious. It consisted of kitchen with a small balcony outside, two bedrooms, a large sitting-room, and bathroom. Eunice had given him the royal tour when they'd arrived. Now he was itching to do something a little more lively. He was trying to remember the last time he'd been laid. It was almost too long to remember.

The longer Eunice sat next to him on that little sofa, legs pulled up beneath her, the more he wanted to get started. If they finished quickly he might have time for a couple of races afterwards, see how Dashy was doing. Then he heard the flush and Eunice came back into the room. Only this time she'd taken her jeans off!

Kevin nearly spilt his drink as he watched her. Now she was sitting on a chair opposite taking off her pullover. Not saying a word. Smiling at him. She was wearing a white bra to go with the panties, small breasts that didn't look too special. Now she was standing up and turning her back to him. What was this, some kind of floor show? Stripping to the sound of Phil Collins on the stereo. He watched her unhook her bra, let it fall to the floor. Then she slipped her fingers into her knickers and inched them down slowly over that great ass of hers. Kevin could feel his breath speeding up. He was nearly bursting out of his jeans as the ass was revealed and the panties fell to the floor. Then she leaned over, put her hands on the back of the chair, opened her legs a bit – and waited.

*

Eunice was on the carpet smiling to herself. Poor Kevin. Her little show had worked him up so much he'd only lasted about ten seconds. And that was with a condom. She'd managed to halt him and make him put one on just in time.

'Was that the best you could do?' she asked him. He was lying next to her still panting, still with his shirt on, jeans down at his ankles, trainers still tied up.

'Just wait a few minutes,' he said. 'You took me by surprise.'

'I thought you'd know better than that. I thought you were a man of the world.'

'It's been a long time. I haven't had anyone for several months.'

'Neither have I,' Eunice said.

'It's different for you.'

'That's what they all say.'

'Just five more minutes.'

'Take your time,' Eunice said.

*

The first thing Chris did at work that Monday morning was to phone his head office. He was sitting in The Wine Seller's back room, looking out through the one-way glass at Rachel, getting the call in while Ron had popped out on an errand. Chris was talking to Donna, the head of personnel for the off-licence chain; they had ten off-licenses in the London suburbs and that seemed to warrant a personnel office in Lewisham. If Chris were running the company he'd let the managers pick their own staff. This Donna he was talking to was someone he'd never met, but he knew she was about twenty-two, and she talked to him as if he were about three. One day he would tell her that he'd had more work experience than she could ever hope to have and that he could do her job with one hand tied behind his back. Now she was saying to him 'I don't knoooow,' in that whiny voice she had. Chris had just asked her if he was entitled to some money for clothes damaged from his mugging.

'I've had to throw away the trousers I was wearing,' Chris said, 'and my jacket is nearly ruined. That was a fifty quid jacket, you know.'

'Well, what ruined it?' Donna asked. 'I'm not with you.'

'Oil,' Chris said patiently. 'Oil and petrol. The bloke hits me, I land on the road, and there are car leakages down there. There's no way you can dry-clean that sort of stuff away.'

'I see,' Donna said. 'So how much are you asking for altogether?'

'Fifty for the jacket, and twenty for the trousers. Seventy altogether.'

'I don't knoooow.' There she was whining again. 'I'll have to ask Mr Hemsley. I can't authorise that sort of thing myself.' Mr Hemsley was one of the directors. Chris had met him a few times when Hemsley had been making spot checks of his off-licenses. He was an overweight businessman who smoked foul smelling cigars. Just the sort of bloke Chris detested.

'Well, you be sure to tell him,' Chris said, 'that I saved him two and a half grand. Seventy quid is nothing compared to that.'

'You didn't actually save him anything. He would have got all that back from the insurance. So in fact he'll be seventy pounds out.'

Chris could feel himself getting angry. If he talked much longer to this girl he'd end up telling her to fuck off.

'Well, just ask him, can you?' he said instead. 'Give me a ring back when you can.'

'I'll ask him, but I can't make any promises.'

'I don't want any promises.'

Chris quickly said goodbye and hung up. He walked into the shop. Rachel was at the till watching him but he didn't look at her. Instead he stood looking at the shelves, waiting until he calmed down. He looked at the glittering bottles of wine, the different colours of the spirits, the mixers and soft drinks, and the stacks of beer in the middle of the floor. Even in his bad mood he was subconsciously telling himself what needed to be brought out from the storeroom. He was bloody good at his job and he didn't need the kind of shit handed out from people like Donna and Ron.

He started filling up shelves then and thought about Rachel. If it wasn't for her, he'd be feeling really bad.

When they'd seen each other that morning, the first time since Saturday night, Rachel had given Chris a lovely smile. In the staffroom they'd been awkward together though, Chris wanting to grab Rachel, give her a hug, but not wanting to commit himself to that kind of thing so early in their relation-ship. They should leave the physical side until after work hours. Now Chris couldn't wait for work to end, so he could take Rachel outside, find somewhere private, and give her another kiss.

Chris's thoughts were broken when Ron came back into the shop. He marched up to Chris and said: 'It might be an idea ringing up Gilbey's and seeing where that delivery's got to.'

Ron was standing close to Chris, looking at him with a creased forehead. Ron was the world's worst worrier. The delivery of wines and spirits should've arrived on Friday and here he was, ten o'clock Monday, expecting it to be there already.

'Okay,' Chris said. 'I'll give them a ring.'

He wandered off slowly to the office. Ron never gave anyone a ring himself, always delegated it to Chris. A delivery was always late to Ron. It should always have arrived yesterday. Chris hated using the phone to chase suppliers and reckoned they must dread the sound of his voice when it was nothing to do with him anyway. Things always arrived eventually. What did Ron expect? This was England, for Christ's sake.

Chris sat at the desk behind the one-way glass again and breathed out. He picked up the phone and watched Ron talking to Rachel at the till. Keep away from her you twit, he thought, and then he was talking to Gilbey's. The delivery was on its way. Thank you, Chris said. Sorry to bother you. He put the phone down and breathed out again. What the fuck was he doing working here?

When he walked back into the shop Ron moved away from Rachel.

'It's on its way,' Chris told him in his bored voice.

'Good. I think I'll go and get my lunch now.'

'It's only ten o'clock.'

'I didn't have any breakfast.'

Bugger off then, Chris thought. Go and buy your chicken tikka roll, come back and breath all over us the rest of the day. Ron went out.

Chris set about some boxes, cutting them open and putting bottles on shelves. He carried a duster in his back pocket and wiped every bottle he put out. He liked the way they sparkled in the lights. He felt Rachel's arm slide around his waist.

'He gets up your nose, doesn't he?' she said.

'Does he ever,' Chris smiled.

'Are we going out tonight?'

'I think we'll both need to.'

'Let me give you a hand.' She bent down and started taking out bottles.

They took turns serving and filling the shelves. When Ron was around he didn't like Rachel doing anything but serving. He'd employed her as cashier, so as far as he was concerned that's all she was allowed to do. Chris found this a very degrading attitude, and also very frustrating. Sometimes he would be struggling to unpack a big delivery and Rachel would be watching him from the till, wanting to help but unable to. He'd suggested to Ron that he could do with some help but Ron would always want the till manned. You never know what might happen, he would say. You might be putting out bottles, your back's turned for a minute, and someone walks out with the till. You don't believe me, I've seen it happen. Chris didn't believe that for a second. The bad thing was, since his mugging, Ron had got even more security conscious inside the shop, and this Christmas would be one hard slog, filling up shelves on his own. Wasn't it just last Christmas he'd sworn he wouldn't be there this Christmas?

By the time Ron came back an hour later, the boxes were unpacked and put away. Ron looked at Chris with surprise.

'We have been working hard, haven't we?' he said.

Chris could never figure out what Ron did in his lunch break. Okay, so he would go out and eat his chicken tikka roll somewhere, but that didn't take an hour. He believed he walked around shops the rest of the time, but he hardly ever bought anything. Maybe he was making lists for his wife to buy. Probably too lazy to buy his own clothes. One of those men that got his wife to do it. Chris could never understand that.

'I'll go and get my lunch then,' Chris said.

'Yes, off you go.'

Chris picked up his coat from the staffroom and walked out past Rachel, giving her a wink on the way. He turned right on the High Street and walked to the police station, a hundred yards away. He had only been there once before when a banker had been caught shoplifting in the Mall. He'd been caught stealing clothes but they'd found three bottles of wine as well. It had been Ron's day off, so Chris had to go and identify the bottles, say yes they had come from his shop, and then write out a statement.

Chris walked up the steps and through the swing doors into the station. It was a smallish place, a polished wooden counter separating him from desks, filing cabinets, and two officers. A radio crackled from somewhere. A middle aged officer came over, looking smart in his uniform, and freshly shaved. Probably just starting his shift.

'And what can I do for you?' the officer asked.

*

Chris hit the cue ball with power and potted an impossible red at the far end of the table. He straightened up nonchalantly, as if he'd meant to do it.

'That boys, is how you make a long pot.' He walked to the other end of the table to line up the next shot.

Ralph and Bill looked at each other. 'What're you on?' Bill asked.

'I've found a seventeen-year-old that fancies me,' Chris said. He had just come back to the YMCA after a drink with Rachel and another friendly kiss. He was in a good mood. He lined up an easy black and missed. Then he told his two YMCA friends about Rachel.

'Lucky you,' Ralph said, when Chris had finished.

'What about Liz?' Bill asked. 'I thought you were after her?'

'Too much of a yuppie for me.'

'Who cares? Look at the body on her.'

'Bodies aren't everything Bill.'

'Why not go out with them both?'

'Bill. You're starting to show your character. Rachel's a nicer girl. I feel comfortable with her.'

'Don't you feel old?' Ralph asked.

'No. I feel young.'

Ralph said: 'I went out with a girl once was ten years younger than me. When we walked down the street together, I just felt so bloody ancient. I thought everyone was looking at us.'

'That's because you look so bloody ancient,' Bill said. 'You shouldn't care what people think.'

'I know, but I did. When we talked I felt as if I were her old man. I couldn't go on with it.'

'So you married someone who was five years older,' Bill grinned.

Ralph shook his head. 'That was a mistake, too.'

'Well,' Chris said. 'There's only sixteen years difference between Rachel and me.'

Then the snooker room door opened and Chris's policeman came in, the Dennis Weaver look-alike. He said hello to Chris. Chris introduced him to Bill and Ralph and got his name this time – Detective Sergeant Morgan.

'News travels fast,' Chris said. 'I didn't think they'd find you so quickly.'

'We have radios these days,' Morgan said.

Chris didn't know whether he was joking but he smiled anyway.

'I'll leave you chaps to it,' Chris said, and led Morgan out and along the corridor to the TV room. The YMCA had two TV rooms to save arguments over channels, but the one near the snooker room was the least favoured. It was like a viewing room, rows of armchairs and a TV and video on a high stand. Like being in a mini cinema. Chris switched on the lights and sat in the back row with Morgan. He told him about how he had gone to the bookies and seen his mugger, how he'd seen him again on Saturday night and followed him home.

'You shouldn't be playing the detective you know,' Morgan said. 'Sometimes it can lead to trouble.'

'I thought it was going to on Saturday. When the blonde one crossed over and came back towards me.'

Morgan sat quietly and then said: 'So you want me to go to his house and question this bloke?' He shook his head. 'It would be a lot easier if I knew his name.'

Chris looked at him.

'I can bluff my way through it,' Morgan said. Then he nodded. 'I don't see why not. I'll think of something. But you'll have to make a positive ID on him. You have to be sure. A hundred and ten percent. Otherwise it'll all fall through and I'll look stupid.'

Chris nodded. 'I'm sure. He seems nervous to me. I'm sure if you pressure him, he'll admit it. Then I'll just confirm it for you.'

'Okay. Good.' Morgan stood up. 'I'll be in touch. Meanwhile, don't do any more following.'

'I won't.'

They left the TV room and Chris walked Morgan down the stairs to the front door.

'You know who you remind me of?' Chris said, making conversation.

'Dennis Weaver,' Morgan said. 'Everyone tells me.'

'It's the moustache. And the height.'

'Every time someone tells me that,' Morgan said, 'I swear I'm going to shave the damn thing off. But then I think, it's better being recognised as someone than no one.'

'You could be right,' Chris said.

'I've always hated Weaver,' Morgan said. 'I mean, McCloud was such a hick cop. He had such a stupid image.'

'I can remember watching it but I can't remember much about it.'

'You don't want to. The only decent thing I've seen Weaver in is *Duel*.'

'Where he's being chased by an empty truck?'

'Yeah, but there is someone actually in it. Somewhere, near the end I think it is, you see an arm poking out of the truck window.'

'That's a scary scene.'

Morgan nodded.

They were at the front door now. Morgan said he'd be in touch and walked off. Outside there was a car waiting for him. Chris watched as Morgan walked towards it and climbed in the passenger side. Chris couldn't make out the driver in the dark, just saw an arm poking out of the window. He shivered and went back to the snooker room.

Ten

Kevin and Dashy were in the Carousel amusement arcade in Boroughheath High Street; a small old room with worn carpet, a change cubicle, and throbbing, flashing machines. It was Tuesday afternoon. Dashy was watching Kevin play Robocop, pumping the joy stick with force, looking as though he was going to break it off and walk away with it in his hand.

'She sounds a bit of a raver, this Eunice,' Dashy said. 'Tomorrow, why don't I come along and meet her?'

Kevin grunted. He was concentrating on the game. Dashy leaned on the machine and looked around the room. He recognised some of the other faces: putting money in slots, seeing it disappear for good, listening to noises, blinded by lights. He couldn't see the sense in it really. Horses were a much better game. At least you had the chance of making something out of it. What did you get in here? A few minutes of pleasure and a big hole in your pocket.

'I wish I had your luck,' Dashy said. 'When I went around to Helen's she didn't want to know. Her mother let me in the house and sent me up to her room. That's a good start, I thought. I knock on Helen's door and she looks at me as if I'm a wart. I mean it's Saturday night. People are meant to want to see people on Saturday nights. She lets me in and I sit on a chair while she sits on the bed. I'm feeling so down I just sit there and hardly say a word. She's wearing one of those horrible track-suit things but still looks fanciable. I just want to jump her there on the bed.'

'Damn! Missed the bastard,' Kevin said.

Dashy could feel the machine rocking against his backside. 'Then she starts asking why I came and how do I know where she lives? I tell her she told me. She doesn't believe me. After five minutes or so she's fidgeting and yawning and saying she wants to go to bed. I look at her and say Yeah? She stands up then and asks me to leave. So much for Saturday night romance.'

He turned around to face Kevin. The game was coming to

an end. 'I think I'll give up on her, you know. I don't think she likes me at all.'

Kevin let go of the joy stick, stood back from the machine and looked at Dashy. 'What?' he said.

*

'Where are we going now?' Dashy asked.

'Follow me. We're going to do some more homework.'

They were walking up the High Street towards the Shopping Mall. Kevin was still thinking about Eunice, still hadn't got over that session yesterday. How many times had they done it? Three times. He'd never done it that many times in a row before, had never even thought it possible. Okay, so he'd read in nudie magazines about it, but he'd never believed it. Usually when he'd shot his bolt he just wanted to get as far away from the girl as possible. Sneak over to the other side of the bed and go to sleep. Even better, get out of there altogether and go home. With Eunice it was different though. He'd stayed because he knew he might learn something. And he had too.

Thanks to Eunice, Kevin had missed all the races yesterday. He hadn't seen Dashy at all. They'd done a bit of betting today but Kevin had got bored with it. His mind was on other things. That's why they'd ended up in the Carousel.

At first Kevin was going to tell Dashy how they'd been followed on Saturday night, but then he'd thought no, Dashy would only shit himself, put himself at risk. And then that would put him at risk for Saturday. He'd decided that was the day he would go out and do a better job than Dashy had done. Show him how a pro worked.

'It's getting darker earlier, the more we get into winter,' Kevin said. He looked up at the sky.

'And warmer.'

Kevin nodded. 'It's far too warm for November.'

'It's the greenhouse effect,' Dashy said. 'The earth's atmosphere is changing.'

'If you say so,' Kevin said. 'The darker it is, the better.'

'So you've decided to do it then?' Dashy asked.

Kevin nodded. 'Saturday week.'

Kevin was telling Dashy the wrong date because he didn't want him to know about it until it was all over. He wanted to be able to hand the bloke some money on Monday and say – it's finished. Done. He'd decided to give him a small percentage for giving him the idea in the first place. But all the planning was going to be his. He'd listen to Dashy, find out his mistakes, and then do it all again with success.

'Let's go up here,' Kevin said. He led Dashy up the side street next to Barclays Bank, past the nightsafe and around the back. It was the first time Kevin had really looked at Dashy's escape route – the back of the bank and the side wall. He stood looking at the bank and the building next to it.

'This other building's a DIY store isn't it?' Kevin said. Dashy nodded. There was a pile of wooden pallets stacked next to a door from deliveries of cement and paint. Behind Kevin was the old Portakabin and building rubble from when the new bank was being built.

'I don't know why they leave this Portakabin here,' Kevin said.

'Maybe no one else wants it.'

'They should Porta it somewhere else,' Kevin said. Dashy didn't laugh.

'What I did,' Dashy said, 'I leaned one of those pallets against the wall there, and you can just run, jump on to the pallet, and over the wall.'

Kevin looked at the wall. It was ten to twelve feet high. He'd certainly need a pallet to get over that. He decided to put one by for safe-keeping.

'Come over here,' he said to Dashy. The two of them lifted a pallet and carried it over to a pile of building rubble. They laid it on the ground behind the rubble, out of sight.

'You think that'll be there in another week?' Dashy asked.

Kevin had forgotten he'd lied to Dashy. 'Of course it will,' he said. 'I'll check nearer the time.' He noticed people walking by on the side street, mainly schoolkids going home. 'Let's get out of here,' he said. 'Passers-by can see us. I don't want to have my face remembered by one of them. Show me the other side of the wall.'

Dashy led Kevin to the front of the bank and up the High Street to a left turning. Then another left turning and they were down a narrow street, and there was the wall, the pavement underneath. They stood next to it and Kevin looked up. It seemed even higher from this side. The ground must be built up on the bank side. He had to admit he was feeling some reluctant admiration for Dashy. He imagined the poor bloke jumping over this obstacle, shit-scared, having nearly been caught, getting away without anything for his troubles. He imagined a pedestrian on this side, seeing Dashy in full flight coming over, a bear-like hulk jumping through the night air. That would be enough to put the shits up anyone.

'Did you hurt your feet when you landed?' Kevin asked him.

'Not that I noticed. My ankle hurt when I got home.'

'Where did you go from here?'

Dashy turned and pointed. 'I went down Chapel Road and started walking quickly. I wanted to get as far away from the High Street as possible.'

Kevin nodded. Seemed fair enough. It would be nice to have a car though.

'I wonder if there's any difference,' he said. 'I mean, you weren't successful, so maybe it was easier for you to get away on foot. I'm going to succeed so I wonder if they'll be after me quicker. They probably just let you go.'

Dashy shrugged. 'Who knows? I don't think you'll have swarms of police after you. And I can't imagine shop workers forming a posse.'

Kevin couldn't imagine it either. The more he thought about it, the easier it seemed. Still, it would be nice to have a car. Jump over the wall, have it waiting around a corner somewhere, drive off and have a few beers to celebrate. Buy the beer with the money. But then cars had number plates and no doubt some eager-beaver would note it down. There were so many neighbourhood watch schemes these days. How did criminals survive?

'Show me the route you walked,' Kevin said. They had plenty of time to kill. 'We may as well go over the whole thing.'

*

Detective Sergeant Morgan sat in his police car outside number 17 Avenue Road, and wondered what the hell he was doing there, chasing up a hunch from an amateur detective. He'd been round earlier in the day but no one had been in. Now he saw lights on in the living room window. Let's get in there and get it over with, he thought.

He walked up the short pathway and rang the doorbell. He could see a figure approaching and a man opened the door. Morgan introduced himself and saw the usual look of suspicion. The man was in his fifties, wearing grey trousers, slippers, and a thick cream pullover. Not long home from the office. Ready to unwind in front of *Eastenders* or some other crap.

'I'm just making a routine enquiry, sir,' Morgan said, showing his ID. 'Can I come in for a few minutes?'

The man reluctantly let him in and showed him into a small living room. The TV was on but it wasn't *Eastenders*. Morgan didn't recognise the programme. He had so little time to watch TV he hardly knew what was on these days. He sat in an armchair by a gas fire and got out his notebook. The man sat down opposite on the sofa. Morgan smiled to put the man at ease. It didn't work.

'I'm tracing a bit of information from the public, Mr... er?'

'Bratton. Clive Bratton.'

Morgan noted it down. 'There was an attempted mugging last week near the Shopping Mall, and the person who was attacked thought he identified the mugger around town a few days later. Unknown to me he started following the chap. Not something we encourage, of course. He saw the man come to this house on Saturday night. I'm here to try and find out who he was.'

'Well, he must've got the wrong address then,' Bratton said. 'I'm the only man that lives here.'

'Can you tell me who else lives here?'

'There's me and the wife, and my daughter Helen.'

'You didn't have any visitors on Saturday night?'

'No, none at all. We were watching TV all evening.'

'I see. Well that brings my inquiry to an abrupt end.' Morgan laughed to hide his embarrassment. 'What about your daughter? Did she have any visitors? The man we're looking for is about twenty-five.'

'No, none at all.'

'How old is Helen?'

'Twenty-one.'

'Right.'

'But she rarely has boys around. We don't allow it. Anyone she sees, she has to see down here. We don't allow them up to her room.'

'Sensible.'

'So if she'd had any visitors we would've seen him, wouldn't we?'

'I suppose so.' Morgan looked at Bratton and didn't like him. Why was he defending his daughter? Had she really had someone round that night and didn't want it known? Or had Chris got his addresses mixed up? He'd like to speak to Helen himself. Without Bratton knowing about it. He noticed some family pictures on the other side of the room. He shut his notebook and stood up. 'Well that's about it then. Could I bother you for a glass of water before I leave? I've had a sore throat all day.'

'Sure,' Bratton said. 'Hang on.'

Now that Bratton was off the hook he would bend over backwards to help. Morgan had seen it so many times before. When Bratton left the room he walked over to the pictures on the window-sill. He picked one up, a picture of a dark-haired girl on a motorbike wearing jeans and leather. Helen, he presumed. Now that he knew what she looked like, he could wait for her outside. Catch her before she got indoors with the protective Mr Bratton.

The door opened and Bratton came in smiling, a glass of water in his hand.

'Great,' Morgan said. 'Just what I needed.'

Morgan left the house after a mouthful of water and went back to his car. He got inside and drove down the street until he was out of sight of Bratton's house. Then he did a U-turn, drove back up the street, and parked a safe distance away. He could sit in his car and watch the High Street entrance to Avenue Road, which was more than likely where Helen would come from. He would have to keep his eyes on the mirror as well though, in case she came from the other direction.

Morgan didn't mind waiting, it was all part of the job, something he'd got used to. He preferred this kind of work to the river police, Thames Division, where he'd been the last five years. Preferred it to those winter nights going up and down the Thames hauling out suicides. Compared to that, this was a doddle.

After only fifteen minutes of waiting, Morgan saw a girl who looked like Helen turn off the High Street and walk towards the house. Morgan quickly got out of his car and jogged towards her, reaching her as she was about to enter the front garden. He showed her his ID and led her away from the house, in case Bratton should look out of the window.

Helen was an attractive-looking girl, despite greasy dark hair, and a petrol-smell emanating from her leather jacket, an odour all motorbikers have. Morgan was sensitive to smells and liked his women smelling sweet. During his five years in Thames Division he'd smelt so many decomposed bodies that even the slightest unnatural odour on someone was enough to put him off. He tried not to let it show as he told Helen why he was there. Then he asked where she'd been on Saturday night.

'I was indoors all Saturday evening,' she told him. 'I was watching TV.'

Morgan sensed she was on guard already. Bikers have a natural distrust of police, so maybe he was wasting his time.

'With your parents?' he asked.

'That's right.'

'I've got a witness who said that the mugger, a young man about twenty-five, was seen entering your house on Saturday night. This was about half-eleven. You don't remember anyone visiting?'

'I think I'd remember if someone visited me or not. Especially a man.'

'What about your mother? Would she have any visitors?'

Helen laughed at that. 'My mother getting men visitors? You've got to be joking.'

'Well. You never know.'

'I do.'

Morgan decided he wasn't getting anywhere. Even if Chris's mugger had been to the house, none of the family were going to let him know. Why was that? Were they protecting someone? He doubted it. He felt they were just naturally cagey.

'That's all I needed to know,' Morgan said.

Helen was looking at him differently now. Relaxing, just like her father had.

'Why did you drag me away from my house?' she asked. 'You could've waited for me in there.'

'Your father's rather protective of you. He wouldn't be too pleased if he saw me here.'

'Well, you know what fathers are like.'

Morgan nodded. He had nothing more to say to the girl. He may as well go and waste his time somewhere else.

He walked her back to her house and went back to his car. The smell of petrol was still in his nose.

*

Chris and Bill were sitting in The Sydney Arms – a pub a few minutes walk from the YMCA – when Liz walked in with a friend. Liz was wearing a long brown winter coat with a fake fur collar. Chris hadn't seen her since Friday night, their meal out and their goodnight kiss. She hadn't even been at the bus stop in the mornings. A lot had happened with Rachel since then though, and he didn't feel much like seeing her now.

'Here's Liz,' he said to Bill, and then wished he hadn't because Bill was waving them over. Liz saw them, motioned to her friend, and they came over smiling, Liz looking a little shyly at Chris. He stood up to let her have his seat, and then spent the next few minutes searching the crowded pub for two vacant stools. By the time he'd got them Bill had already bought more drinks.

'So what brings you here?' Bill asked the two girls. The other had been introduced to Chris as Tassie. Was that how you spelt it? What kind of a name was that? She had straight brown hair that curled around her chin. When she took off her coat Chris saw a nice pair of legs under the table.

'This is the road we live in,' Liz said. 'We come down here most nights, don't we Tassie.'

Tassie nodded. 'You've seen us down here before, Bill.'

'You're right. I have. And I must say I'm glad to see you here now.' Bill winked at Chris.

Chris thought, here we go, I'll have to sit and listen while Bill tries to chat up one or both of these two. He sipped his beer and watched Bill in action. Bill was amusing most of the time, but with women around he raised his game, so to speak. Chris was sure both girls saw through it. They were just playing him along. Bill was fifty years old after all. Surely they were interested in younger men. Chris was sitting next to Liz and wanted to apologise for not calling her. She didn't seem too worried or angry with him. She was giving him the same smiles Bill was getting.

As it neared closing time, Bill suggested they buy some beer and all go back to the YMCA. Chris was surprised when the two girls agreed. Tuesday night and they both wanted to party.

They bought two four pint cans of beer and walked back to the YMCA. Chris had a chance now to talk with Liz.

'Where have you been these last two mornings?' he asked her.

'I had to go in early. I was probably on the train before you were out of bed.'

'The early bird.'

'I had some extra work I had to get through. Tomorrow I'm going in later.' Chris noted the remark. He looked up ahead and saw Tassie and Bill with their arms linked, laughing at something as they walked. Probably one of Bill's jokes. Chris wondered when and where the evening was going to end. Then he felt Liz's arm slide through his.

'I've thought about you a lot,' she said.

'Have you?'

'That sounds like you haven't been thinking of me.'

'I have,' Chris said. 'Every day.'

When they reached the YMCA, Bill stopped everyone from going in. They hid to the side of the reception doors.

'Now listen, girls,' he said. 'Visitors aren't allowed after eleven o'clock, so we'll have to smuggle you in.' He turned to Chris. 'I'm going to pretend to Harry I've locked myself out of my room. When you see us walking away, go up the stairs to the first floor and then along and down. Give him time to let me in, though.'

Chris nodded.

They watched Bill walk in and talk to Harry the security guard. Harry followed Bill out of the foyer, his master-keys dangling from his right hand. Chris led the girls in and over to the stairs on the right. They walked up to the first floor.

'We'd better be quiet,' he told them as they sneaked along. 'You never know Harry. He might make a detour back from Bill's room.' Chris wasn't worried about any of the other residents seeing them, it was only the management who didn't like visitors. If you were found with a girl in your bed, you were liable to be told to leave within the week. Looking for another place to live was a hassle Chris didn't want to face right then.

They made it safely down to Bill's room after Chris had checked every corridor and staircase beforehand. It reminded him of old western movies, sending the scout beforehand to warn of Indians. Once Bill had shut the door behind them, they all started laughing.

Then they opened the beer.

*

Chris was coming out of the toilets, one o'clock in the morning now, feeling the worse for drink. The bright corridor lights were too much for him after the gloom of Bill's room. Bill had only put the bedside lamp on, so as to make the atmosphere more sexy.

After opening the four pint cans of beer, they'd listened to Bill's old Frank Sinatra records, and then he'd put on his video and they'd watched home movies. Bill had his own video camera and he'd taken lots of film at his health club: rich women in leotards working out, fat business men climbing out of the swimming pool posing with a drink in their hand. Then group pictures in the bar, people laughing and getting drunk. Chris couldn't see the sense in health clubs. You sweat away on an exercise machine and then drink your weight back on in the bar. He guessed Bill was trying to persuade the girls to make a visit. Get them alone in the sauna. They had been keeping their voices down in case old Harry wandered past on his rounds and heard girly laughter. How would they get out of that one? Blame it on the TV? Say that Bill's doing one of his impressions?

Chris saw Liz coming down the corridor then, heading towards him. She looked good to him, wearing jeans and those nice short crimson boots, a blue pullover. They walked up to each other and rather than dodging, walked straight into each others arms. They kissed in the corridor, under those lights, Chris's head spinning from the beer, thinking to himself – any minute Harry's going to come around the corner and catch us.

'Let's go to my room,' he said, and led Liz away by the hand.

Inside his room, Chris drew the curtains and they started kissing again. Then they undressed each other. The radiator had been going full blast all day so they'd be able to do it naked, on top of the bed, the way Chris liked it. As their clothes began to fall away, Chris compared Liz to Amanda. He hadn't made love to anyone since Amanda. How would it feel? He looked at Liz's body, the breasts a lot larger than Amanda's, and the stomach swelling out a bit more. Liz had suntan lines where her panties had been, but not up top. Her legs were meatier too, nice strong-looking legs with a lovely dark patch in between.

Chris was naked too now and wondering if Liz was comparing him to anyone else.

But when she got hold of him and started moving, he forgot about Amanda and thought only of Liz.

Eleven

Chris sat with his egg, bacon, and headache. That was one good thing about the YMCA – no matter how much you'd been drinking the night before, you didn't have to make your own breakfast the next day. Stagger into the canteen, have a choice of cereals or something fried, or both, plus orange juice, tea or coffee.

He saw Bill coming in, dressed in jeans and grey sweatshirt, looking showered and reasonably sprightly. When he'd collected a tray of food, he came and sat with Chris.

'I didn't expect to see you here,' Bill said. 'I thought they would've thrown you out by now.'

'For what?'

'For having a girl in your room.'

Bill started attacking his food. 'I get a knock on my door about six-thirty. This female voice is saying, "Bill, Bill, are you awake?" I know who it is, so I open up. It's Liz come to get her coat.'

Chris shrugged. 'She had to leave early. She wanted to get ready for work.'

'She only stays about ten seconds and then she's gone. Ten seconds and I've missed half an hour's sleep.'

'You were on your own then?'

'Of course I was.'

'What went wrong?'

'When you didn't return, Tassie started getting worried. She knew what you two were doing and thought I'd expect that of her.'

'You would.'

'So she waited ten minutes or so and then left. Left me high and dry at my own party.'

Chris reached over and patted Bill's hand.

'And you've got a girlfriend already. How are you going to explain away this one?'

'I won't tell her. I haven't slept with Rachel yet. It's not as if I've been unfaithful.'

'It's being greedy, that's what it is.' Bill looked over at the door. 'Here comes your friend.'

Chris turned around and saw Detective Sergeant Morgan walking in. Instead of coming over to their table though, he walked straight to the serving area and got some breakfast. Then he came over and joined them. They said good morning to him as he sat down.

Bill nodded at Morgan's breakfast. 'Did you have to pay for that?'

Morgan shook his head. 'You get a lot of benefits in this job.'

'All right for some.'

Morgan looked at Bill.

'Bill's pissed off,' Chris said. 'Sulking.'

'Nothing worse than a sulker,' Morgan said. 'I like people who get it out in the open, tell me things and then let me follow it up. I prefer it though when their information's correct.'

Chris looked at him. 'Did something go wrong?'

Morgan nodded. He couldn't speak because he had a mouthful of food.

'Is this secret, or can anyone listen?' Bill asked.

Morgan swallowed. 'There's no secrets because I came back with nothing.'

'What happened?' Chris asked.

Morgan washed out his mouth with coffee. 'I went to 17 Avenue Road, and talked to a Mr Bratton first off. He was a cagey devil and said no one had been in his house that night, except for members of his family. That's just him, his wife and daughter. I didn't believe him, so I waited outside until his daughter came home. She didn't like me either, and like father like daughter, as they say, said there hadn't been any visitors.'

'Shit,' Chris said. 'So my mugger doesn't live there. He did go in there, though. They were lying to you.'

'I have to tell you, I agree with you. But why?'

'My mugger's a very close friend of the family?'

'I doubt it.'

'What the hell's this all about?' Bill asked.

'I'll tell you later,' Chris said. He sipped his coffee and looked at Morgan. At least Morgan believed him.

'I think the father is being over-protective of his daughter,' Morgan continued. 'And I think the daughter just didn't like me. She was one of those motorcycle people. Leather jackets and dirty hair. I could tell you what her record collection would consist of without even seeing it.'

'All heavy metal,' Chris said.

'Anything to do with the law and she would automatically clam up. A natural reaction.'

'Probably had dope in her pockets too,' Bill said.

'You'd get good odds.'

They sat and looked at each other. Morgan finished his breakfast and sat back looking satisfied. Chris wished he could walk in places and get free food.

'So what happens now?' he asked.

'Nothing,' Morgan said. He wiped his hands on a napkin. 'That my friend, is the end of the investigation.'

'Well, I'm not impressed.'

Morgan raised his eyebrows. 'You don't have to be.'

Chris looked bitterly into his empty coffee mug. He'd felt so sure his information would lead to an arrest. Now it would lead to nothing, because a stupid father and daughter wanted to play games with the police.

Morgan was standing up now, ready to leave. Was this going to be the end of it?

'You know, you get good food here,' Morgan said. 'Maybe I'll come back for more sometime.'

Chris felt confused. What was he going on about?

'And if you should happen to find out anything else…' Now he was tapping his nose. 'Let me know.'

Chris nodded and Morgan left.

Bill had a puzzled look on his face. 'There's one thing I want to know,' he said.

'What?'

'How did Liz get out past Harry this morning?'

Chris switched his mind back to the previous conversation. You could be in the middle of a nuclear war and Bill's mind would still be on women.

'I told her to walk out and smile at him. I presume that's what she did.'

'I wouldn't have the balls to do that. That girl must have a lot of guts.'

Chris drained the last of the tea from his cup. 'Well, I can tell you one thing Bill. She certainly doesn't have any balls.'

*

Rachel leaned on the till counter and watched Chris putting bottles away. At the back of the shop, behind the one-way glass, she could make out the shape of Ron moving around. He was most likely watching them both, seeing how they were acting. She wondered if he suspected anything yet. Would he try and split them up if he found something was going on between them? She knew he'd be jealous. Ron had being making passes at her ever since she'd started at the off-licence. She hated the days when Chris wasn't there, when it was just her and Ron alone for eight hours. On those days he'd actually let her put bottles away, and then there he would be squeezing past her in the aisle, making sure he rubbed against her in some way. That kind of thing made her fume, but what could she say? If she confronted Ron, he would just deny it, put on that dumb 'who me?' expression, and walk off. He was that sort of person. Slimy slime.

She looked at Chris bending over. He was in a funny mood today. A good mood, but different. Hungover and tired. He said he'd been drinking last night. Why hadn't he asked her along?

The previous night she'd told her older sister, Tracy, about him. Tracy had met Chris in the shop, and although she quite fancied him herself, didn't think the two of them were suited.

'He's too heavy for you,' she'd said. Rachel had asked her what she meant by that.

'He's too intense. He thinks too much. He's only after your body. When he's had that what will you talk about? He's thirty-three and you're only seventeen.'

'You think I'm thick, is that it?' Rachel had said. 'Actually I have more exams than Chris does.' A whole lot more in fact. She had two A-levels while Chris had left school long before he could take any. He had a complex about it too.

'I'm not talking about exams,' Tracy had said. 'Oh, forget it.'

But Rachel couldn't forget it. That's why she was thinking about it now.

The only time she felt Chris was 'too heavy' for her was when he started talking about music. He would mention groups and singers from the sixties and seventies she'd never heard of. He would make references to particular lines in songs that meant nothing to her at all. All she knew about was today's charts. The only records she had were by Madonna and The Pet Shop Boys. Chris didn't like either of them although he had admitted he fancied Madonna. But then, didn't every bloke she'd ever talked to?

She actually felt a bit sorry for Chris. She knew he didn't like the off-licence business, but what else could he do for a living? He had no qualifications or trade. She thought he should get back into music in some way. Maybe he could become a radio disc jockey. He had a pleasant voice, and certainly knew music. Maybe she'd suggest that to him next time they went out. But when would that be? He hadn't mentioned anything so far today.

*

Chris took deep breaths when he stepped out of the off-licence at lunchtime. His head was giving him terrible problems and he just wanted to go home and sleep. Plus he felt so guilty being around Rachel all the time. He'd hardly spoken to her all morning.

He crossed the High Street and entered the Drop In Café, finding a table by the window. A middle aged waitress came over and took his order. A nice big fry up, his second of the day, would straighten him out. And a big glass of milk.

It was the first time Chris had been in the little café – small red tables and fixed chairs, a counter at the back where the food appeared. He was sure this was where Curly had watched him from. What a great view of the Shopping Mall entrance! You could sit here and take notes. That's if you didn't choke first. Everyone in there seemed to be smoking. Stuffing down their food and leaving lit cigarettes burning away in ashtrays. Chris had smoked once, in his mid-twenties, but had come to think of it as a waste of money. And time. He could taste his food better, too.

He looked at the people passing and wondered what they did with their days. He was feeling more than a little pissed off with Morgan. If the man was any more laid back he'd fall over. He didn't seem to care one way or the other whether they caught Curly, and yet he had hinted he'd follow up if Chris found out more. But what more could he find out? Would he have to get Curly's name, address, and telephone number? He thought he'd already done that, but he'd have to start again. What a balls-up it was. If only Curly had gone straight home instead of visiting that family, they'd probably have him by now. Well, he would just have to try and track him down again and get a bit more information. Concrete information.

His food arrived and Chris ate quickly, thinking he should be in the bookies really, seeing if Curly was in there. He finished his glass of milk and asked for another. He wiped up the egg yoke with a slice of bread, paid his bill and left.

When Chris opened the bookies' door he was met by another cloud of smoke. He saw that Curly wasn't in there but hung around for a few minutes and looked at the TV screens anyway. He had to admit he liked the place. He liked listening to the commentary and looking at the different coloured lettering on the screens. He dragged himself away and stood in the street again, wondering where to look next.

He looked up and down the High Street and decided to walk down to the old part of town. Get away from the crowds.

He walked past small tatty shops wondering how they still stayed in business now that the Mall was starting to milk them dry. He felt some sympathy, but the shops did look out of date; tired-looking exteriors and unimaginative window displays. There were a lot of boarded-up shops already, and the pubs were being refitted systematically, as if a wind of change were gradually blowing down the street. When the Asda monstrosity was finished, it would complete the bastardised look once and for all.

Chris had walked this same route on Saturday when he'd been following Curly and his blonde friend. He came to the Broadway video shop, a new construction, and decided to have a look inside. In the window was a cardboard cut out of Sylvester Stallone carrying a machine gun, ready to destroy. Next to him was one of Arnold Schwarzenegger in his latest science fiction epic. Chris had never seen such a big video shop.

He pushed open the double doors and walked inside. The shop was at least thirty yards long and about half that wide. He was the only customer. On the right was a long counter where two men in their forties were sitting. They were wearing short-sleeved white shirts, grey trousers, and red ties, waiting for something to happen. There were TVs mounted on the walls and one of the men was watching *Fawlty Towers*, sitting there squinting at the screen about twenty feet away. They both gave Chris a bored look and he nodded at them.

Chris started looking at the racks, trying to find a video he wouldn't mind watching, but it was mostly martial arts and sex as far as he could see. And more cardboard cut-outs. There was Kevin Costner in *Dances With Wolves* next to Anthony Hopkins in *Silence Of The Lambs*. He had to get out of there before he started laughing. What a waste of space! But at least he'd found another place where Curly might hang out. He'd have to try there again sometime in the evening, when maybe it would be a little busier.

He crossed the street and walked back to work on the other side. After another hundred yards he found something else – The Carousel amusement arcade. It was just a converted shop with a painted sign above. Not too enticing. Chris didn't have time to stop but stored it for future reference. Worth another visit sometime. He carried on walking, feeling a lot better than when he'd started his lunch break. His headache had eased and he had a few more things to work on in the evening and during future lunch breaks. A few more places where Curly might hang out. He quickened his pace, so he wouldn't be late back. Ron would only start complaining. Then he slowed down. Sod Ron. He relaxed and started looking in shop windows.

*

Kevin had been looking in shop tills.

Doing some legwork. Trying to find out who was taking the most money.

The Boroughheath Shopping Mall consisted of thirty-five shops, which included a Marks and Spencer, a BHS, Woolworth's, and Safeway's. It had three walkways which converged on the central fountains with their seats and plastic plants. Kevin worked his way methodically around the Mall, starting at the main entrance – where Lasky's was – and finishing at one of the side entrances. Then he went home, sat in his room and wrote it all down....

> *ELECTRICAL SHOPS. They take a lot of money in big amounts, but I think because the amounts are so big, most of it's credit cards. No use to me. And they always send blokes out with the money anyway.*
> *BOOKSHOP. Too quiet in there.*
> *OPTICIANS. I'd need my eyes tested if I robbed them. A busy place but not much cash exchanging hands.*
> *JEWELLERY SHOPS. A lot of money going in there, but could be all paper again. One to keep in mind. Have to pick the right jeweller because some of those shops are as dead as can be.*

SHOE SHOPS. Quite a lot of cash I would think.
Again, pick the right one. Some of them are dead.
CLOTHES SHOPS. Similar to the shoe shops. A lot
of cash if you pick the right one. And there's always
girls working in there so it's girls that bring the
money out.
LEATHER SHOP. Not busy enough.
SAFEWAY'S, BHS, MARKS AND SPENCER,
WOOLWORTH'S. Forget them. Security picks it up.

When he'd finished, Kevin underlined <u>JEWELLERY</u> and
<u>CLOTHES</u>. He decided to spend most of the next day just con-
centrating on them, trying to memorise faces. It was more com-
plicated than he'd thought. He could understand how Dashy
had left it all to chance. Standing by the pub in the dark, waiting for the right person to come out, pumping himself up, getting ready for that moment, and then picking someone who
didn't even work in the Mall but a shop further down the road.
It was easily done. Maybe that's what he should do. Just say
bugger it and see what happens. Pot luck. But he didn't want to
do that. He wanted one good score so he could get out of that
house. Get away from his old man for good.

Kevin went downstairs and made himself a cup of tea. His
father wouldn't be home until late. He imagined having the
house all to himself like this every night. No one to bother him.
Or maybe a flat like Eunice's. Now wouldn't that be good?
Maybe he would use the stolen money for a house deposit,
instead of trying to place a few good bets. Now wouldn't that
be a laugh? Walk into an estate agents and put down a deposit
of stolen money. It was worth thinking about. Put up with his
dad until he got his licence back, start working again, and then
buy a flat like Eunice's. He fancied somewhere like that, somewhere comfortable he could take girls to when he wasn't on the
road. But maybe he should think about it when he'd got the
money safely in his pocket. He had to do that first.

Kevin took his tea upstairs to his bedroom, sat on the floor
cross-legged, and looked at his piece of paper again. Now, was
there anything he'd missed?

Twelve

'So how's the job hunting going?' Kevin's father asked him the next morning.

'I thought you'd gone to work,' Kevin said, surprised to see the old bugger still sitting in the kitchen.

'I've got a gut-ache. I'm waiting an hour to see if it settles down.'

'Don't go in.'

'I've got to. I've got a lot to do.'

'Because it's getting near Christmas?'

'That's right. Now don't change the subject.'

'How's the job hunting going? It isn't going. It's always there.'

'You haven't found anything? I could get you a job at the post office over Christmas.'

'I've done it before.'

'Do it again.'

'I'll think about it.'

'Don't think about it too long. There are plenty of others waiting to do it.'

'Yeah, fucking students. That's one of the reasons I'm not keen on it.' Kevin sat down at the table.

'They're harmless enough,' his father said. 'They just think they know it all.'

'You said it.'

'Think about it, anyway.'

It amazed Kevin that his father still pushed him on the subject. Had he forgotten their little fight six months earlier? He thought that would put the fear in him for good, show him who's boss. But no, here he was again, pushing. Always pushing. Like an animal butting itself against a fence. A stubborn old goat.

'You remind me of a goat,' he said to his father.

*

Dashy had jobs on his mind, too. He spent the morning down the Job Centre trying to keep a low profile. The previous evening he'd had a telephone call from Helen which had started him worrying again. His heart had been pumping when his mother had told him it was a girl.

'Dash?' He had recognised Helen's voice straight away.

'That's me.'

'What the hell are you up to?'

Dashy's heart stopped pumping.

'What do you mean?'

'I had the pigs round here last night, asking about you.'

His heart sank.

'Asking about what?' he had barely managed to say, trying to keep his voice low as he stood there in the corridor, his parents watching TV in the next room.

'Someone followed you to my house on Saturday night. The pig seemed to think you were mixed up in something.' Then Helen's voice had started getting louder. 'Now listen here. I don't want to ever see you again. If you're in trouble, I want no part of it. I want no part of you anyway. Who the hell do you think you are coming around at that time of night? And getting me involved with the law!'

'I didn't know I was being followed.'

'So that makes it okay, does it?'

'No.'

'I'm getting through.'

'I'm sorry.'

'It's too late for that.'

Dashy didn't know what to say.

'Just don't talk to me if you ever see me again. All right?'

Dashy still didn't know what to say.

'All right?'

He was just about to say yes when the line went dead. Click. Right in his ear.

Now he was sitting on an orange armchair in the Job Centre waiting his turn. He was applying for a labouring job, advertised on one of the job cards on the wall. In this Job Centre you had to fill in a piece of paper and stick it on a spike on the serving lady's desk. Now Dashy was on his third cigarette as he watched the spike, making sure the woman took the bottom piece of paper off and not the top one. The woman would take about five minutes with each applicant, before sending them to an interview with a Job Centre card in their hand. That always angered Dashy. Half the employers didn't even look at the card anyway. What did the Job Centre think it was? A reference? A letter of introduction? Did they think applicants were so thick they couldn't introduce themselves?

'Mr Dash?' said the woman at the desk.

Dashy stood up and went to sit in front of her. She was middle-aged, grey haired, wearing a brown suit. Dashy watched as she flipped through a box on the desk that held all the reference cards. She pulled one out and said, ' Building labourer?' Dashy nodded.

'If I could just take a few details…'

Dashy told her his work record, leaving out the bit about getting sacked.

'Why did you leave?' she asked.

'I wanted a change,' Dashy said.

The woman looked around the Job Centre, the people looking at the boards, the people waiting, and then back at him.

'Well, this is certainly a change,' she smiled.

Dashy could've strangled her. Stupid woman sitting there making jokes at his expense. Stupid woman who didn't give a shit, doing this job so she could earn a bit more money and spend it on clothes, clothes to impress her friends. She could stick it right up her…

'I'll give them a ring,' she said.

Dashy watched her pick up the phone and begin dialling. Then she watched him as it rang. Looking him over.

'Hello? Mr Turner, please.'

They looked at each other.

'Mr Turner?… This is the Boroughheath Job Centre. I've got a young man here interested in your labourers job… Yes, the labourers job… When was this…? I see… I wish you'd let us know… You did…? Someone must've forgotten to take the card down… Okay. Sorry to have bothered you.'

She hung up.

'I'm afraid the job went three weeks ago, Mr Dash. We must have forgotten to take the card down. Or we weren't informed.'

Dashy nodded at the woman. This had happened to him before. She had no apology in her face. He didn't know why he bothered with Job Centres. It was better to look in the local paper for a job. Go directly to the source instead of coming through these inefficient people. He stood up. The woman was already calling out the next person's name. She didn't even say goodbye to him, so Dashy didn't say anything either. He walked out of the smoky atmosphere and stood on the street. Then he walked over to The Carousel.

*

Chris was already in The Carousel.

He was playing a fruit machine very slowly, trying not to waste too much money, taking an early lunch because he was so sick of being cooped up in The Wine Seller. Out of the corner of his eye he saw the door open and when he turned, he saw it was Curly. Their eyes met. It would've looked bad for Curly to walk straight out again and Chris watched as he walked over to one of the driving machines and sat down in the seat behind the steering wheel. He put some money in the slot.

Chris hadn't seen Curly since Saturday, the night Chris thought he was following him home. It was almost like seeing an old friend again.

He walked over and stood behind him. Chris saw his reflection in the screen as it lit up and a picture of a highway in the desert came on.

'Good luck,' he said.

Curly nearly jumped out of his seat.

'What?' he said, turning his head, but Chris was directly behind him so there was no way he could see him without getting out of his seat.

'You're on,' Chris said.

Curly said, 'Oh,' but not quickly enough, because his car had already started and smashed into a tree. The machine made crashing noises. He grabbed hold of the steering wheel and drove back on to the highway.

Chris smiled and looked down at Curly's head, the short wiry hair in tight knots. It would be so easy to reach down and put him in a head lock. Hold him tight and make him struggle a bit, ask him why he'd mugged him. Chris could feel those kind of emotions rising to the surface. He could pick up that empty beer bottle lying on the carpet there, wack Curly over the head and run off. No one would go after him. Instead he moved from behind and stood next to Curly. Curly was trying to drive and watch him at the same time, his eyes darting everywhere. He was having a hard time keeping the car on the road and every few seconds there'd be the crashing sound and a small explosion would light the screen.

'You're a terrible driver,' Chris said.

Curly nearly jumped out of his seat again. 'Why don't you fuck off,' he said.

'Okay.'

Chris walked behind Curly again and put a hand on his shoulder. He squeezed it hard and said, 'Just keep on trying.' Curly flinched.

And then Chris walked out of the door, the sound of another crash echoing behind him.

*

Dashy looked over at the shutting door. He took his right hand off the steering wheel and saw it was shaking. He struggled out from behind the machine, having trouble with his bulk, then walked quickly to the door and out.

He looked up the street and saw the bloke walking away. He started jogging after him. He didn't quite know what he was going to do but he wanted to have a confrontation, find out what was going on. He couldn't spend the rest of his life being followed everywhere. It would drive him crazy.

He came up behind the bloke and grabbed him by the arm.

'What's your game, then?' Dashy asked, out of breath from the short jog.

'What's my game?' the bloke said. 'What's my game? That's a good one.'

Dashy stood there not knowing what to say. The bloke was looking at his hand on his arm so he let go.

'I want something in return,' the bloke said to him then.

Dashy didn't know what he meant. He stood there trying to think of something to say. This was the first time he'd seen the bloke up close. He was an inch or two shorter and thinner; a good-looking bastard who'd probably have no trouble picking Helen up. But there was also something hard there too. Dashy could see it the way his eyes were narrowing. He also noticed a slight lump on the left cheek. They were standing close together in the cold air, their breath lapping against each others faces.

'Something in return for what?' Dashy asked him.

'You know what. I haven't got time to talk about it here. Meet me outside the shop at six. Okay?'

Dashy didn't like the way the bloke talked to him. As if he were giving orders.

'Okay?' he said again.

But Dashy had to find out what was going on.

So he said okay too.

*

Chris walked back to work feeling pleased with himself. Good, he thought. Now we're getting somewhere.

When he arrived back at the shop, Ron asked him where he'd been. Chris said he'd bumped into a friend he hadn't seen for a long time.

'You should talk to them after work hours,' Ron said.

'That's what I'm going to do. That's what I was arranging.' Chris looked at his watch. 'What am I, ten minutes late? For Christ's sake, lighten up.' Then he went to the staffroom to take off his coat.

For the rest of the afternoon Chris tried to work out what he was going to say to Curly. What did he mean exactly when he'd told him he wanted something in return? What the hell could Curly give him in return? Money? Booze? A video machine? Or maybe let Chris punch him on the cheek, give him a swollen face like his. Chris didn't know, but at least he knew he was now in a powerful position and could start threatening him. That's if Curly turned up.

The afternoon went slowly, just Chris and Ron in the shop. It was Rachel's day off. Chris hadn't seen Liz since he'd slept with her on Tuesday night, and he found his attention switching back to Rachel. Tomorrow he'd invite her to the YMCA for the whole of Sunday. Take her out for a pub lunch and then back to his room. See what would happen.

At six o'clock Chris said goodbye to Ron, and saw Curly waiting off to the side. He walked over to him. They nodded at each other.

'Which pub do you fancy?' Chris asked.

'Anywhere but The Angel,' Curly said.

Chris agreed.

They walked in the opposite direction where there was another pub just newly re-fitted. It was next to a new car park and Chris thought it highly unattractive. He'd never been there before and doubted if many people had. A pub next to a wide open space. He told Curly his name but didn't offer his hand. Curly introduced himself as Leo Dash.

'Most people call me Dashy,' he added.

'Okay Leo,' Chris said.

In the deserted pub Chris bought Leo a pint and they sat at a table. Chris could see Leo felt uneasy, hunching over his drink, drawing wet beer patterns on the table with his finger. Chris didn't know what he was feeling, but he certainly wasn't feeling bitter. Since the meeting at The Carousel when he'd felt slightly aggressive he'd calmed down. He'd had the afternoon to think things over. He didn't want to reach over and pummel Leo's face. All he wanted was for Leo to admit that it had been him. Then he would give his information to Morgan and let the law take its course.

'What do you do for a living?' he asked Leo, to get the conversation started.

'Nothing. I'm on the dole.'

'For how long?'

'Eight months.'

Chris nodded. 'I was on it once for a year. I got fed up with working and didn't want to do anything. Then I got fed up with doing nothing and wanted to work again. But there aren't so many jobs these days.'

'You can say that again.'

'Plus you've got the Job Centres, of course. They prevent you from getting work too.'

'Fucking useless places.'

'So how do you survive? You live at home?'

'Yeah. My dad lets me have money sometimes. Or I do some betting.'

'I saw you in there once.'

'In where?'

'The bookies.'

Now Leo was looking at him with caution. Chris thought he could lead him into a confession quite easily.

'I don't remember seeing you in there,' Leo said.

'Come on. I know you saw me in there. You virtually jumped out of your skin. You were with that blonde friend of yours.'

'Why would I jump out of my skin?'

'Because you saw me.'

'So?'

'Because I'm the one you mugged a few weeks ago.'

'What the fuck're you on about?'

'You know,' Chris said, and picked up his beer. He let the silence hang there. If you used a little silence people got uncomfortable and then they tried to fill it.

'Why would I want to mug anyone?'

'Because you don't have any money. That's a pretty good reason. Don't worry about it, I'm not going to hit you or anything. I'm not going to hand you in either. I just want to hear you say it.'

'Say what?'

'That you did it.'

Chris let the silence in again. Leo was moving uncomfortably in his seat. Chris found himself smiling.

'You know you throw a pretty good punch. I've still got a lump here. Can you see it? The doctor says it'll go eventually. I hope it does. It still feels stiff though. It hurts when I laugh.'

Leo still wasn't saying anything.

Chris carried on. 'When I first had it examined the doctor said I had a crack somewhere and the air I was breathing was blowing it up like a bicycle tyre. You find that funny? Have you ever been compared to a bicycle?'

Leo shook his head. Chris could see a guilty look coming on his face.

'Then I stayed indoors for two days. It's funny the looks people give when you walk along the street. I mean, I think of myself normally as a pretty nice-looking bloke, and I get my share of looks. Then I was on the street getting looked at for a different reason. It was weird. I felt like a freak. Still, it does us all good to be brought back down to earth for a while .'

Leo mumbled something then.

'Pardon?' Chris said.

'You shouldn't have resisted then,' Leo said.

And there it was.

*

The Boroughheath Shopping Mall stayed open until nine o'clock on Thursday evenings. Because the Mall had only been open two years, it was still relatively unknown in the area, and had to have advantages that other centres didn't have to attract new customers. The management committee had thought hard and come up with the late Thursday evening idea. Okay, so other shopping malls opened late on that day too, but how many of them opened until nine o'clock?

Amanda thought the idea preposterous.

Here she was walking around with her father, and the whole place was virtually deserted. She didn't mind that of course – it made shopping a lot easier – but she felt sorry for the staff who had to work so late for a few extra sales.

It was just over a month to Christmas, so Amanda was taking advantage of the Mall to get some shopping done in peace. She had got in from work at six-thirty, suggested to her father that they go out, and here they were.

Already he was asking if she'd nearly finished.

'I knew I shouldn't have brought you,' she said. 'Don't you have some shopping to do?'

'No,' her father shook his head. 'I'll leave it until later. It's too early to be thinking of Christmas.'

'Yes, I know you. You'll leave it so late that I'll have to get everything for you. Well, this year you'll have to do it yourself.'

'I will do it myself. Don't you worry.'

Amanda doubted that very much. Over the years she'd had to buy many last minute presents because her father had 'forgotten'. And then she had to pester him to get the money back. She'd never known anyone so stingy. So why did she do it year after year? She didn't know. And it would be worse this time because she was living at home again.

'I'll believe it when I see it,' Amanda said. 'I'd better buy a few more things to allow me more time in December.'

She led her father into Marks and Spencer and bought three more presents. She was wondering whether to buy Chris anything too. Would he buy anything for her on this first Christmas since their split? If he did it would be a CD. Chris's imagination hardly stretched any further.

When she'd finished in M&S, and had as much shopping as she could carry, Amanda relented to her father's grumblings and his empty stomach and agreed to go home. They walked to the High Street and headed for Amanda's car; she always parked in a side street, refusing to pay exorbitant fees in the indoor car park. Maybe she'd inherited some of her father's stinginess.

They piled all the bags on the back seat of the car and drove slowly down the High Street. Then they stopped. The traffic was snarled-up, grinding its way around the one-way system. Amanda put the car in neutral and they sat for a minute waiting. They were opposite a pub and as Amanda glanced over, she was surprised to see Chris coming out with someone she didn't recognise. She thought she knew all of Chris's friends – that wasn't too hard, he didn't have many – but this was a face she didn't recognise. She watched the two of them say goodbye and Chris walk along the opposite pavement, his hands deep in his pockets, his head down low, as it always was.

Amanda wound down her window and tooted the horn.

'Do you want a lift?' she called out when Chris looked at her.

Then he jogged across the road towards them.

Amanda had to get out of the car to let Chris into the back. She heard him saying hello to her father. As they settled into their seats the traffic started to move again.

Amanda looked at Chris in the mirror and asked, 'Who was that you were with?' She noticed his sudden glance at the mirror.

'Just a friend.'

'Oh? Which one?'

'You don't know him. Someone who comes in the shop.'

Amanda didn't believe him. Chris had always been a bad liar.

'We do have our little secrets, don't we?' she said, feeling annoyed.

Chris didn't reply. Her father turned in his seat and looked back at him.

'Did you watch the match last night?' he asked.

Here we go, Amanda thought. Shall I let them both out here?

Thirteen

Eunice was hiding in the public bar.

Normally she worked in the saloon bar and crossed through to the public only if they were busy and needed extra help. But she had just seen Kevin sitting in his usual position at the bar in the saloon, and she was thinking, stew him, let him sweat a bit.

She hadn't seen him since she'd taken him home with her that Monday afternoon. Poor boy was sure to be still recovering. She'd enjoyed her few hours of superiority. She'd shown him a few things he'd obviously never done before, maybe hadn't even thought were possible. Well, she liked to put people like him in their place, macho men who thought they were it. And now look at him. Now he'd got his strength back he'd returned for more. Well, let him wait. I'm not running after him.

*

Kevin sipped his pint and went through the newspaper, marking horses.

He didn't plan on going to the bookies though, was just killing time until Eunice came over and he could chat her up. What was she doing in the other bar, hiding from him? Probably scared of him after his performance on Monday, scared she'd have to go through it again and maybe enjoy it as much the second time around. Kevin started to feel good just thinking about it. He was definitely ready to take her on again.

Yesterday he'd spent most of the time hanging around the Shopping Mall again. He'd decided, after his in-depth analysis, to rob one of the women's clothes stores. There were two reasons for this: one, he thought they took quite a lot of cash during the day; and, two, the staff were almost always girls and would be a push-over to rob. So he'd spent the day going around them all a few times: Next, Top Girl, Fantasy – such stupid fucking names – plus a few others, trying to get people's faces into his head, memorising them for when he saw them walking through the Mall's big sliding doors, carrier bag in hand. And it hadn't been an easy task, either.

First of all, in a woman's shop, a man sticks out like a sore thumb. There he'd be, standing around racks full of dresses and undies – he'd like to see Eunice wearing a few of the things he'd seen, garter belts especially – trying to look natural, with all the women mingling around. In the first few shops Kevin had just walked through quickly, as if he were looking for a lost girlfriend. Then he'd be back outside in a few minutes thinking, hang on, this is too quick, I hardly got a look at the staff. So then he'd started hanging around the changing-rooms, pretending he was waiting for someone. But that was dangerous, too. He'd found himself getting mesmerised.

Those changing-rooms were very interesting places to watch. He'd be standing behind a rack of something finding he couldn't tear his eyes away. A girl would go in, draw the curtain, usually leaving a small gap at the side. He could see the curtain moving as garments were removed, and then see flashes of legs and arms as the girl struggled into something two sizes too small for her. And then she'd come out to show her boyfriend and the dress would be so tight, it would be hugging her breasts so you could make out practically everything. Or it would be so loose a strap would slip off and give him a flash of shoulder. One time a girl had just pulled off a tight pair of jeans and she'd pulled her panties half off too. Kevin caught a glimpse of her bending over, half the crack of her sweet little white ass visible. He'd had to get out of the shop then. Either that or risk ending up in the changing-room with her.

In one shop he'd hung around a little too long and an assistant had come over and asked if she could help. He'd been so engrossed watching he hadn't seen her come up. The sound of her voice startled him.

'What?' he'd asked, stalling.

'I wondered if you needed any help,' the assistant had said. Young and blonde with a perm. Lots of paint on her face. Didn't they all look like that?

'No,' Kevin had said quickly. 'I'm just waiting for someone.'

'You've been waiting for fifteen minutes,' the girl had said, trying to get clever with him.

'Have I? Is there some limit on waiting time, then?'

'No. It's just that I think she would've come out by now, don't you?'

Kevin had given her a knowing smile. 'Well, you know how

long they take. She told me she'd be in Working Girl and that I
was to wait for her.'

'But this isn't Working Girl. That's next door.'

'Is it?'

Later, Kevin had to smile at that. That had been a bit of quick-
thinking, pretending he was in the wrong shop. He'd walked
out of there and hadn't gone back. Had watched the shop on his
next circuit from outside, standing opposite. But the girl who'd
caught him, he wouldn't forget her face. He'd like it to be her he
knocked over Saturday night, but that would be too risky. Even
a girl as dumb as that could put two and two together.

When he'd finished looking around, Kevin had gone to the
coffee shop in BHS and written down all his thoughts. But
what had he come up with? Nothing really. He found his
descriptions of girls all sounded the same: blonde and tall,
blonde and good-looking, blonde and rough, overweight, too
much make-up, or I wouldn't touch it with yours. How the hell
could he separate that lot, standing in the dark, heart pounding
away, waiting to get it over with? He decided he'd have to trust
to memory, use the old brain, that's what it was there for. And
use it now, because here comes Eunice.

'Well, well, well,' she said to him as she walked past. 'If it
isn't lover boy himself.'

Kevin had to smile at that. She'd noticed then. He watched
her pick up a beer bottle and snap the top off. The beer erupted
from the bottle and Eunice poured the foaming liquid into a
glass. It reminded Kevin of something.

'Where have you been hiding yourself?' Eunice asked.

'I've been recovering from Monday,' Kevin said. 'It's been
sore.'

'Well, That'll teach you to keep it hidden away.'

'I have no control over it.'

'No?'

'It's got a mind of its own,' he said, grinning.

'I always thought that's where your brains were.'

And then she was walking off! What the hell was wrong
with her?

*

When there was only half an hour left until closing time,
Eunice walked over to Kevin and asked what he was doing
afterwards.

'I was hoping you'd ask me that,' he said, that smarmy look on his face. 'What took you so long?'

Eunice ignored the question. 'You'll have to wait outside until I'm finished, though. I've got a lot of glasses to clean,' she said. 'I don't want the manager to think I've got a toy-boy.'

'That's what I had to do last time, remember? It's so bloody cold out there.'

'I thought you were tough.'

'I am.' He gave her a quick smile and then shut it off quickly. 'How about giving me your car keys and letting me sit in that? You'll be half an hour in here.'

'Okay.'

Eunice didn't mind that. The car park was at the side of the pub and no one would see him there. But why was she going through all this? She didn't like Kevin much, so was she really that frustrated? No. It was just that she liked to go to bed with someone twice. The first time was usually too quick and awkward and the second was always more interesting. A bit more experimentation could come into play. The other person was much looser and it was more fun. Then when that was over a decision about the relationship could be made. She knew her decision would be to dump Kevin. She doubted if he would mind. He was just after casual sex, too.

'I'll get my keys in a minute,' she told him.

'Have you got a radio in there?'

'Of course.'

'Good. That'll help pass the time.'

Eunice shook her head and went to serve someone. The guy couldn't bear to be in his own company for thirty minutes. If she didn't have a radio, she'd probably walk out and find him ripping up the upholstery. Or emptying the ashtray on the floor. Christ. Where have all the grown-ups gone?

*

Kevin sat in Eunice's car twirling the ashtray, before sticking his finger in it. He poked around amongst the cigarette ash to see what he could find. What did he expect to find? A used condom?

He looked at his watch. She should be out soon. He was already bored with Radio One. For a start he couldn't stand the DJs, and secondly, he couldn't stand the music. The DJs were like overgrown schoolkids the way they ranted on. He wondered if they spoke like that in everyday life. Jesus, if he spoke like that, he'd get laughed at every place he went. And the music! When he'd been driving long distance lorries, he'd never had the radio on, always preferring cassettes. His favourites were Bob Seger and Thin Lizzy, but anything was better than radio music and that trivial, chattering bullshit. He fiddled with the tuner, skipping from song to song to cut out the talking altogether.

But then Eunice came out. Shit, she had some body on her! Walking across the gravel car park towards him. Wearing high heels and beige cords. Tight beige cords. Right up her middle. And a short brown jacket. And a handbag slung across her shoulder. He'd have to keep his eyes on that for later.

He reached over and opened the door for her.

'You surprise me,' Eunice said as she got in.

'Why's that?' he asked.

'You never struck me as the kind to have any manners.'

Kevin laughed. He had to laugh. Sometimes he wasn't sure whether she was joking or being serious. Well, he'd show her he wasn't such a dumbo when they got back to her place.

'I'm full of surprises,' he told her.

'I'll bet,' Eunice said.

And then she turned on the ignition.

*

'Just supposing,' Chris said, 'someone gave you a couple of grand. Or you found a couple of grand. What would you do with it?'

'In what way?' Rachel asked.

'Well. Would you put it towards a house. Or buy a car. Or go on a cruise. Or move to another area and start a new life?'

Chris was sitting at the desk with Rachel on his lap, looking through the one-way glass into the shop. It was Ron's day off and they'd decided that instead of a tea break, why not a cuddle break? They'd been sitting that way for ten minutes and not a soul had come into the shop. It might be Friday, but that didn't mean it would be busy.

'I'd buy a car,' Rachel said. 'I'd buy something flashy and drive to all the pubs and make my friends jealous.'

'But you can't drive.'

'I'd use the leftovers for lessons. Buy the car first. Imagine that. Learning to drive in a Ferrari or something. It would be fun turning up for your test in one of those.'

'A Ferrari costs more than two grand I'm afraid.'

'Does it? Oh well.' Rachel had her fingers in his hair. Twirling it around. 'I wouldn't buy a house anyway.'

'Why not?'

'I'm too young.'

'I thought people started off younger these days. Haven't your parents brainwashed you into getting married and settling down yet?'

'No. I don't think they want me to ever leave home. Anyway, Tracy'll be the first. I'll think about it when she goes.'

'How about a bed? You could buy a good one of those.' Chris had been amazed when Rachel had told him she slept on the living room sofa every night. Or rather, one that converted into a bed. Her parents' house was a two bedroomed affair and Tracy had the only spare room. Rachel had to wait each night for everyone to go upstairs before she could make her bed up. She didn't seem to mind much either. She was used to it, except for the odd twinge of back pain in the mornings. Chris had once slept a year on a bed-settee and knew the feeling. He hated the things.

'There wouldn't be any room, would there? I'd have to put it on the lawn.'

'You could buy a tent, too.'

Chris shifted a bit in his seat. Rachel was beginning to get heavy. He pulled her towards him and kissed her. He couldn't leave those lips of hers alone. She had a knack of pursing them as if she were trying to suck him in.

'So what would you spend it on?' Rachel asked when they'd stopped.

'That's easy. I'd pack in this job and move to another area. Start all over again.'

'And leave me behind?'

'I guess so.'

'Thanks a lot!'

Chris could see someone coming into the shop now.

'The tea break ends,' he said.

Rachel got off and went into the shop. She hadn't been too happy about that last remark of his. Still, what did she expect? Marriage?

Chris stood up himself and then sat down again. Better wait a few minutes. The trouble with those kind of tea breaks was that parts of you responded in noticeable ways.

*

Kevin watched Eunice walk naked from the bedroom. He heard the bathroom door shut and quickly got out of bed. He hurried into the sitting-room and picked her handbag up from the armchair where she'd left it. He opened it, took out her car keys, and slipped them into his jacket pocket in the hallway where it was hanging. He heard the toilet flush and went back to the bedroom.

'Listen,' Eunice said when she came back in. 'I've got to do some things before work tonight. Can we call it quits?'

'You want me to leave?'

'In a word, yes.' Now she was sitting on the bed, turning towards him. 'In fact, I don't think we should see each other again. I don't think it's going to lead anywhere.'

Kevin could feel himself getting angry. What the fuck was she on about?

'You mean you just had the best screw you'll probably ever have and now you want to get rid of me?'

'I wouldn't call it the best screw I've ever had.'

'Of course it was. Whose was better?'

'I'm not going to tell you about my sex life.'

'Ha! I am your sex life.'

Now she was getting off the bed and starting to get dressed. Kevin got out of bed and walked over to her. He caught her by the arm and pulled her towards him.

'Listen, lady. When I split up with someone it's me that does it, okay?'

'How can you? I just did it.'

He poked her in the ribs and gripped her arm tighter.

'No you didn't. I just did it. Now say after me. You just did it.'

'Get lost.'

'Oh! Fuck me and now fuck off!'

He twisted Eunice's arm and threw her on the bed. She was just wearing knickers and the sight of her was starting to get him excited again. He jumped on top of her and pinned her down.

'Now tell me. You just did it. Four little words. You – just – did – it.' He put his face up close to hers and breathed in it. Her body was tense under his. He liked the frightened look on her face.

'You just did it.'

'Like you mean it though.'

'You just did it!'

He smiled and nodded, his breath coming quicker.

'That's right,' he said, trying to get his breath back to normal. 'I just did it and now I'm going to leave.'

He stood up and as Eunice bent forward he gave her a backhand slap across the face. She fell back on the bed.

He started getting dressed. He was feeling nervous, not thinking clearly. He had to get out of there sharp, before anything else happened. He'd got what he'd come for. The car keys. Now, just get out of there and away. He could hear Eunice getting back into bed behind him. As quiet as a lamb now he'd shown her who was boss. Giving him the elbow! No one ever did that to him!

When he was fully dressed he turned around to face her. She was lying in bed with her knees up and the sheets pulled to her chin. And were those tears he could see on her cheeks?

'Well Eunice, it's been great,' he said. 'Sorry we had to part like this but that's the way it goes. I'm not the type to get involved in a serious relationship.' She wasn't saying a word. Looked a bit scared. 'Well, I'll be seeing you.'

He opened the bedroom door and left.

*

Friday night and Chris was alone. Alone in his room, lying on his bed in the YMCA. Listening to a Kris Kristofferson tape. He wished the YMCA was a hotel instead of a YMCA. Then, on nights like this, when there didn't seem to be a soul around, he'd be able to sit in the bar and at least talk to the barman or whoever else was stuck there.

He felt his stomach rumble.

He'd taken Rachel for a drink after work and had missed out on his evening meal. If you knew you were going to be late you could book a meal to be saved, go in the kitchen when you got back, and bung it in the microwave. But he hadn't booked one that morning and so felt under-fed. Still, he had Sunday to look forward to. Rachel had agreed to catch the bus over about midday. They'd go to a pub and then come back. Chris was wondering if he could sleep with two new women in the space of a week. Liz on Tuesday and then Rachel. It was something he'd never achieved before but reckoned it was on the cards. Even though he loved women generally, apart from Amanda, he'd never had any long term relationships. He just wasn't geared towards it. So at the end of the day, all he had was statistics and the memories of those he'd been with. And he'd been with a fair few. He didn't think it was bad to think in that way. He always seemed to be able to split up on reasonably good terms and still stay friends. That was the way to do it. There was no reason why people should get hurt. It wasn't worth it.

He got off the bed and put the kettle on. Now Kristofferson was singing *Me and Bobby McGee*. Life on the road. Maybe he should go to America. There was more romance about the place than England. Especially if you liked music.

He rummaged in the cupboard under the sink to see if he could find anything to eat. He found a chicken chow mein cook-in-pot. He hated the things but it was better than nothing. He ripped off the lid and poured in boiling water. Stirred it around with a teaspoon and watched the stuff thicken. Stodge. Or more realistically, a tub of shit. He sat down at the desk with a cup of tea. For dessert he could have a few biscuits.

He thought back to his meeting with Leo. Or Dashy, as he liked to be called. A weird chap. It was hard to believe someone like him could organise a mugging. He didn't seem to have the brains for it, but what brains did you need to be a mugger anyway? You just pump yourself up and go for it. A quick decision. Go in, all guns blazing, and hope to come out the other side.

Once Chris had got the confession out of Leo, he had become resigned, almost as if he were ready either to turn himself in or just give up on everything. And by everything, Chris meant life. The bloke looked so depressed he could be on the verge of doing something silly to himself. Like jumping in front of a train. He didn't seem the type to slash his wrists. He looked like a jumper. Off a building or in front of a truck. One final gesture. Chris believed wrist-slashers were the ones who only did it for sympathy. A few quick cuts and a drop of blood on the bathroom floor. Just enough to frighten mummy and daddy. No, Leo wasn't one of those. He was a jumper.

So then, Chris had to convince Leo that he wasn't going to turn him in. Get him away from those suicidal thoughts. But he had told him he wanted something in return. He didn't say what exactly, didn't even know himself, but he wanted something in return for his bashed face. Why should he suffer all that for nothing? That's how they'd left it, Leo walking into the night, trying to think of some compensation for Chris. Chris was sure he'd come up with something. He had to, because Chris could still be a bastard and change his mind. Morgan would like the information, for sure.

Chris threw the empty cook-in-pot into the wastepaper bin. He could imagine the stuff sliding down his stomach. He opened a pack of biscuits and started on them. He looked at his watch. In another two hours he could go to bed.

Fourteen

Dashy roamed Boroughheath High Street hoping he'd bump into Kevin. The street was filling up with Saturday morning shoppers. The small street market was open and men were shouting in coarse south London accents, announcing low prices on socks and handkerchiefs, fruit and veg, and Christmas wrapping paper. Dashy often wondered about these street-sellers and how much money they made. Were they rich or were they scraping a living? Were they born into it, or was it something you applied for? It was the only job he could think of he'd never seen advertised in the paper or at the Job Centre. Where did these people come from? Maybe they just sprouted out of the streets. One day he'd have to stop and ask. Before that though, he'd have to get used to just walking past them. He didn't like the way they shouted in his ear. If he was half asleep, they put him on edge. And he couldn't say anything back because they'd only say something smarter, loud enough so everyone could hear.

Dashy hurried past and went into the Broadway video shop. The place was virtually deserted, just a few kids giggling over the blue movies. Although Kevin lived a mile away, Dashy knew he went there for his videos. He wasn't there now, though. He looked behind all the stands just to make sure, and then went back on to the street.

He headed for the Shopping Mall.

Looking for Kevin on a day like this was mostly a waste of time but there was nothing else to do. Although he was friendly with Kevin he'd never actually been to his house, so he couldn't catch the bus to Blackfen and see him there. He knew the estate Kevin lived on with his father, but didn't know the house number.

Dashy tried The Carousel and then the bookies. It was going to be one of those days.

What he wanted to see Kevin about was Chris. The guy was after something, but what? Dashy wondered whether he should've admitted the mugging or not. Well, he hadn't actually admitted it, Chris had wheeled it out of him. Talked him into a corner, so before he knew it he was almost admitting things. But he'd still never said, 'I did it'. But Chris knew and that was the worry. And now he wanted something in return. Dashy presumed he wanted money but Chris hadn't actually said so. Maybe he wanted a new TV or hi-fi, or a tip on a horse. How the hell did he know? He wanted to find Kevin and ask him, at the same time dreading what Kevin would say. He'd call him an idiot for going drinking with Chris and for walking into his trap. Dashy thought about their meeting in The Carousel and how he'd run after Chris. If he hadn't done that, he wouldn't be in this position now. But it was done. Too late.

Somehow things just didn't seem to be getting any better.

*

Kevin was at home watching Saturday morning kiddies programmes. His father was at work, so he had the whole house to himself. He was lying on the sofa in his pyjamas and dressing-gown, a cup of tea on the floor in front of him. The TV might have been on, but he wasn't taking much of it in. He was thinking about the day ahead, and the immediate task of going over to Eunice's and taking her car. That shouldn't prove too difficult, unless she happened to come out while he was doing it. He'd have to take that chance.

He'd been watching TV for two hours. Somehow it just mesmerised him on a Saturday morning, maybe because he was always waiting for the afternoon to start, for midday and *Grandstand*, and then the horse racing. Saturdays always fell into this routine. Kiddies programmes, then sport, then the dead hours between five and seven before Saturday evening – the best evening of the week – got under way. Then, as the evening turned into Sunday, hopefully a decent midnight movie on the box. It always started and ended there on the sofa. Well, wasn't life strange? But today would be different.

He stirred himself at ten minutes to twelve. He went upstairs to the bathroom, stripped off, and stood under the shower for fifteen minutes. He needed a wash to wake himself up, and also to make his body feel loose for the exertions that lay ahead. He got out and dried himself, dressed in jeans and sweatshirt, and was back on the sofa in time for the beginning of *Grandstand*. He watched the line-up of sport to come in the afternoon, set up the video for while he was out, put on his grey anorak with Eunice's car keys in the pocket, and walked out into the cold afternoon air.

The bus stop for Welling was right outside the estate on the other side of the road. Kevin crossed and then had to wait twenty minutes for one to come along. During that time he counted four going the other way. He stamped his feet and swore under his breath, one time swearing a little too loudly and getting a look from an old lady who was also waiting.

The bus ride took ten minutes and Kevin got off and walked straight to where Eunice lived. The block of flats was four storeys high and Eunice lived on the second. Her car would be in the garages, off to the right. Kevin walked up the drive and unlocked the door of garage number six. He was out of sight of Eunice's front windows and the only way he would be caught was if she came down or saw him driving away. He wasn't worried about that, though. He believed he'd scared her enough yesterday to stop her from doing anything foolish.

Eunice didn't work in a pub Saturday lunchtimes so Kevin guessed she'd be sitting in her flat having lunch. When he brought the car back around six o'clock she would've already left for her evening shift and would probably report the car stolen when she got to work. The only way it would be spotted earlier was if she decided to go out shopping in the afternoon. Kevin didn't know her well enough to know whether she'd do that, but it was a risk he was willing to take. He thought that by the time the police got the paperwork done and started looking for the car he'd still have it back where it belonged.

Kevin opened the driver's door of the Cortina, climbed in, and turned on the ignition. The old car came to life on the second try and he reversed out. Then he had to get out and lock the garage door. If Eunice didn't have a spare set of garage keys then she'd never find out if her car was gone anyway. It was looking better all the time.

Kevin drove slowly down the driveway, not bothering to look back up at Eunice's flat, and out on to the road. Then he drove to Boroughheath. He took the car into the Shopping Mall's indoor car park and parked on the second level. It would be safer there for half a day than parked in someone's street. All it took was a nosy neighbour to take down the number. Kevin locked the car behind him and went down to the shopping area.

Then he had about four hours to kill.

*

The bottle of German white wine tasted sweet and Eunice reckoned she deserved it.

She was sitting at her small kitchen table eating paté and French bread, knocking back the wine and trying to lift her spirits. She was feeling depressed and had to do something before facing work in the evening. Saturday night was the most lonely night of the week to be working, and after what had happened with Kevin, she really didn't want to go to work at all.

The whole thing had been a mistake.

She could see it so clearly, but now was usually too late. Well, in the future she'd be a damned sight more careful about the kind of men she picked up. She should've dumped Kevin after their first sex session and not gone for the second believing it would be better. For a few minutes yesterday she'd been really scared, thinking he was going to rape or beat her up. She'd been slapped around before but had never been confronted with the mad look in Kevin's eyes, the kind of look that could so easily signal a slip into something more serious, maybe even murder. It made her shudder to think about it. She was lucky to be sitting there in one piece but that didn't make her feel much better.

Because now she had the additional problem of her missing car keys.

Just when she was getting used to knowing that she wouldn't have to see Kevin again, she'd gone into her handbag an hour earlier for some face cream, and noticed the keys had gone. She'd sat down in an armchair and started to cry, almost reaching bawling state like a little girl, feeling so miserable she couldn't remember ever feeling so bad. Not even when Michael had finally left her, the evening he'd packed his clothes into two suitcases and said he was buggering off. Fifteen years of marriage gone just like that. That had been bad, more a feeling of shock though, while this new feeling was one of being totally alone, of being abused by a potential psycho and not having a friend she could turn to or talk to.

Maybe she should go to the police. But what could they do? Kevin hadn't done anything apart from hit her once and he probably wouldn't get arrested for that. And as for the car keys, he may have just taken them by mistake. Everything was so fuzzy, she couldn't remember for sure whether she'd put them in her handbag when the two of them had arrived together, or if she'd given them to him for some reason. Had he closed the garage door for her and pocketed the keys then? She couldn't remember. Or had he stolen them once they were inside the flat? But when? On his way out after their row? Eunice thought with dread that maybe he'd taken them so he had an excuse to see her again. Bring the keys back into the pub one lunchtime and try and make it up with her, hang around the bar in his usual place and hope she'd invite him home. She couldn't bear the thought of that.

Anyway, whatever happened, she didn't have the use of a car for the weekend. She'd have to catch a bus to work and a taxi back. And how much would that cost her? It wouldn't be worth going to work if she had to shell out for that.

She stood up, feeling a little light-headed now, and went to the telephone in the hallway. She dialled The Bricklayers Arms and asked for Bob, the manager. As she waited she could hear the lunchtime pub noise, and it made her feel even more friendless. Then she heard Bob's gruff voice.

'Bob? It's Eunice. I'm not coming to work tonight. I don't feel too good.'

'Oh. Nothing serious I hope?'

'No. Just women's problems.'

'Well, no doubt we'll manage without you. We'll struggle, but we'll manage,' Bob chuckled.

'Thanks. I should be in tomorrow.'

'You come in when you feel like it. There's no point working if you're struggling. We'll manage.'

Eunice almost started crying. It was good to hear a friendly voice again. She almost changed her mind and said she would come into work. But then Bob was saying he had to run, and Eunice put down the phone. She went back into the kitchen and finished the last of the wine. Then she went to the fridge and got another bottle out. Later she'd walk to the video shop and rent herself a nice film to watch. Something romantic. Lie down on the sofa under a blanket and slowly get drunk. Even the worst situations had their compensations.

*

Dashy was walking towards the Shopping Mall, after one unsuccessful bet in the bookies, when he saw Kevin looking at video machines in Lasky's window. He walked up behind him and said, 'I've been looking for you all day.' He enjoyed the way Kevin jumped at the sound of his voice. Mr Tough Guy taken by surprise.

'What for?' Kevin asked abruptly, an annoyed look on his face.

Dashy noticed the look and said, 'Nothing really. Just haven't seen you for a few days.' He'd been meaning to tell him about Chris but after the frosty welcome, it didn't seem such a good idea.

'Well, I'm still the same. Haven't grown horns or anything since I last saw you.'

'You haven't been in the bookies. I thought you were ill or something.'

'The day I need to go to the bookies every day, I may as well give up.'

'Sounds good coming from you. You were always there every day.'

'Everybody needs a change. You should try it sometime.'

Then Kevin was turning from the window and walking away. Dashy turned to follow. What the hell was eating him? Just because he'd made him jump.

'You fancy a coffee?' he said when he'd caught up with him.

'You buying?'

'If you like.'

Kevin looked at his watch. 'Okay.'

'Don't force yourself.'

'Let's go to BHS.'

Five minutes later they were seated at a table in the BHS cafeteria and fifteen minutes after that Dashy was watching Kevin walk out, having drunk his coffee and smoked a cigarette just about as quickly as it was humanly possible. They'd talked about football and racing. Dashy finished his cup and decided to follow.

By the time he got to the top of the escalator Dashy could see Kevin's legs disappearing at the bottom. He ran down the escalator and saw Kevin walking through the main doors and on to the walkway. He jogged through the store, getting a suspicious look from a security guard, and jogged some more until Kevin was within easy distance. Then he saw him pushing through the exit-door that led up the stairs to the toilets and car park.

Dashy climbed the stairs behind Kevin, hearing his footsteps above on the stone, and listening for the sound of a landing door opening. He passed the floor where the toilets were and could still hear Kevin climbing above him. Then some kids came hurtling down the stairs, and Dashy had to lean back against the wall to let them through.

When they arrived at the third floor, the stairs ended and led out to the first floor of the car park. Dashy sprinted up the rest of the way, walked cautiously on to the parking level, and saw Kevin disappearing up a ramp to the next level. He couldn't figure out where Kevin was going because Kevin wasn't allowed to drive. So maybe he was meeting someone up there. He followed up the ramp.

On the next level Dashy saw Kevin walking through parked cars until he came to a light blue Cortina. He dodged behind a concrete pillar as Kevin looked around and unlocked the car. He stayed behind the pillar and watched as Kevin drove off, the Cortina disappearing down the Exit ramp. Well, well, well, he thought. Now, where did he get that old banger from? And what did he need it for?

Dashy stepped out from behind the pillar and leaned for a moment on a white Mercedes. Then he pushed himself off to walk back downstairs. A loud siren started wailing making him jump a foot in the air. Fucking car alarms! He swore at the Merc and walked quickly away.

*

Kevin had changed his plans.

It had been bad luck bumping into Dashy like that, but maybe it was a blessing in disguise.

His original plan had been to do the same as Dashy had done and wait at the junction of the nightsafe road, by The Plough. Now he knew that Dashy was around town, he had abandoned that idea. It would just be his luck to be spotted by Dashy and have him wander over and ask him to go for another cup of coffee.

So now Kevin had decided to hide at the back of the bank, just in front of the old Portakabin, behind a seven foot wall. He could poke his head around the corner of the wall and watch people walking towards the nightsafe which was only about fifteen yards away. When the time came, he would have to walk to the nightsafe, grab the money, then run back the way he'd come, jump over the other wall and away. He'd already set the pallet up against it and tested it. It seemed firm enough. And the Cortina was waiting on the other side.

The only problem with this hiding place was when someone walked by, either heading to the Shopping Mall or coming from it. Kevin would then have to duck behind the wall, and he feared that while he was hiding, he might lose time if one of his targets suddenly came into view. Still, improvisation was no doubt a major part of crime, and if that's what he had to do, then that's what he would do. He stood huddled in his coat and tried not to think of the cold or the butterflies causing havoc in his stomach; he felt a great need to empty his bowels and hoped he could hold on until the job was over. Otherwise he'd have to do it right there behind the wall or the Portakabin. He couldn't see any comfortable-looking rocks.

Kevin had come to the hiding place at about ten-to-five. He reckoned that by half-past, one of his targets would've come out and he'd be long gone. He'd brought a dark blue woollen hat with him and had it pulled low over his head. In the evening gloom he didn't want anyone making out his blonde hair.

At ten-past-five Kevin recognised two of the girls from Next coming across the High Street. They were one of his targets. But as the girls chatted on the traffic island, they were joined by a couple of blokes from another shop (they looked like one of the jeweller's shops) and they all came over together. Kevin swore and ducked behind the wall. With four people around it would be far too risky, and two blokes together might take it into their heads to go after him. Be patient, he thought. Hold on to your bowels and be patient.

*

After seeing Kevin drive off in the Cortina, Dashy spent another hour walking around the Mall, thinking. Thinking and calming down from the shock of the car alarm. He could only come up with one conclusion.

At five o'clock he walked up the High Street and turned left behind Barclays Bank. He walked down the narrow side road to the wall he'd jumped over two weeks earlier. Bingo! There was the Cortina parked underneath it. He looked around the street for somewhere safe to hide.

*

Kevin had to go.

He left his wall, ran back into the dark, and squatted behind the Portakabin, near a pile of rubble. He quickly took down his jeans, squatted, and felt immense relief as the shit poured out. It only took a minute but then he had to find something to wipe himself with. He settled for the wrapper from an empty bag of cement. When he'd got his jeans back up he hoped there hadn't been any loose cement still on the wrapper. He jogged back to his hiding place, feeling a lot better.

After that he was impatient to get it over with.

A few minutes later a couple of more girls came down and headed towards the nightsafe. Kevin recognised them from She Girl and decided this would be the one. It was nearing five-thirty and he was running out of alternatives. The only problem was, both girls were carrying carrier bags.

As the girls neared the nightsafe, Kevin pulled his woollen hat down further, came out from behind the wall, and started walking up the road towards them. He'd have to wait until they were just about to put the money in before he reached for a wallet. He couldn't just snatch a carrier, in case it was empty.

Walking with his head down, he neared the girls as they unlocked the safe. But they saw him coming and huddled together hiding their carriers between them. Kevin walked past and stood by the cashpoint machine, rummaged in his pockets as if looking for a cashpoint card. He could feel his chest pounding, like it was about to burst, and, looking sideways at the girls, he saw a night wallet being lifted out of a carrier. He darted suddenly towards them, pushed one of the girls out of the way, and grabbed the wallet just as it was about to be dropped into the safe. Both girls started screaming, and Kevin pushed them aside and ran quickly off down the road. Then he spotted the old woman.

She was walking up the road towards him, moving slowly as old people do. She must've been right behind him as he came from behind the wall, must've seen the whole thing. There was nothing much he could do about it, so Kevin side-stepped her, not worrying about any resistance. He was wrong. As he passed, her arm came up and he felt her handbag come smashing into his face. There wasn't much force behind it, but it was enough to throw him off stride and he almost dropped the wallet. With a stinging face and watering eyes, he rounded the wall and ran towards the pallet. This was the tricky part, the bit that would go wrong in bad dreams. He sprinted towards the pallet and placed his foot on the top of the wood.

*

Dashy was hiding in the alleyway opposite the wall, between two garages. He heard screaming from the other side of the wall, and then watched in amazement as Kevin's head popped up, followed by a hand clutching a leather night-wallet, closely followed by the top half of Kevin's body. Dashy watched as Kevin dropped the wallet by mistake, and saw it bounce once and land under the Cortina.

Kevin was panting hard as he straddled the top of the wall and then dropped over to safety. Dashy felt the nerves in his own stomach as he willed Kevin to get away. Then he saw him looking around for the wallet. He could see Kevin starting to panic, looking around him, wondering where the fuck it had got to. Despite himself Dashy started smiling. What an idiot he looked!

Then Kevin was on his knees spotting the wallet under the car. Then he was crawling under and pulling it out.

Kevin had left the car unlocked, so the door was no problem. Dashy felt some sympathy though as he watched Kevin fumbling with the ignition. It seemed to take an age for him to start it. Then he over-revved and nearly stalled as he pulled away. Dashy watched as Kevin drove off. He came out from between the garages and started to panic.

He realised he'd better get away himself, in case somebody thought he was the mugger.

Fifteen

'If we hurry, we should just make it,' Chris said to Rachel.

'Will they let me in?'

'Yeah. I'll just have to pay for you, that's all. As long as you don't mind eating in a canteen full of men. Or boys I should say.'

'It could be interesting.'

They were walking back from Elmhurst High Street after what was turning out to be a minor disaster. Chris had met Rachel off her bus at twelve o'clock and they'd been to four pubs trying to find just one that did food. Chris had reckoned without it being Sunday, the one day of the week when pubs don't cook. By then they'd had three drinks and two packets of crisps each. Some lunch date. He was leading Rachel back to the YMCA where, if they got back before one-thirty, they could still get a proper Sunday roast.

'You can always look back and say this was the first date you'd been taken to a canteen.'

'I don't mind, really.'

'You wait until you see the food,' Chris joked. 'I'll have to sign you in when we get there. That'll slow us down a few minutes.'

'Let's run then.'

They jogged the rest of the way, Chris puffing badly behind Rachel. Rachel did a workout every morning which was one hundred percent more exercise than Chris managed. Although he didn't smoke any more, he still got out of breath easily if he exerted himself. He'd often wished he could be there to see Rachel's workouts. She'd told him about them often enough. She would get up at seven, slip on a skimpy leotard, and do a few stretching exercises. Then she'd go out on the back porch, even in winter, and do about fifteen minutes of skipping. She'd come back indoors, do some more stretching to warm down, and then take a shower. That's why she always came into work looking pink-cheeked and healthy. And that's why she was waiting for him at the YMCA doors as he puffed to a halt in front of her. He doubled-up to catch his breath.

'Come on,' Rachel said. 'It's nearly one-thirty.'

They went into the foyer and round to the reception cubby hole. During the day it was manned by one of the youngsters who worked there. Chris looked through the hole and saw it was empty.

'Let's go and eat,' he said. 'They're probably having lunch too.'

Chris led Rachel to the canteen and pushed through the swing doors. As they walked in he felt every eye turn on them – it was a rare sight to see a girl in the canteen.

'I bet you've never had so much attention,' Chris said.

Rachel was blushing as they walked up to the serving area. 'I've never felt so naked.'

'There's about a hundred blokes in here. Most likely, ninety-five of them are undressing you right this minute.'

'Only ninety-five?'

'Plus me.'

They grabbed some cutlery and trays and Chris nodded at Marvin, an odd-looking man who worked in the kitchen and was waiting to serve them. Marvin had a hare-lip which affected his speech, so Chris found it hard to understand what he was saying most of the time.

'Can I pay you for one extra?' Chris said, indicating Rachel.

'Of cauth,' Marvin said. Chris took some change out of his pocket and paid.

'What would you like?' he asked Rachel.

'What would you recommend?'

'Well, there's beef or beef. Roast potatoes or roast potatoes. Cabbage or carrots or both.'

'I'll have the beef and roast potatoes and both.'

'I'll have the same.'

They watched as Marvin filled their plates, heaping on the food with scant regard for presentation. They took a scoop each of gravy from the metal containers and poured it over their piles of food.

'I hope you're feeling hungry,' Chris said. 'Now for drinks: you can have tea or coffee, milk, or orange squash.'

'Orange, please.'

Chris took a milk and they went to look for a table. He didn't like coming into the canteen this late because it was hard finding a seat. On other Sundays he was always one of the first in. He looked for Bill and Ralph, noticed Ralph at an already full table and nodded at him. Bill was probably sitting in a pub somewhere. He rarely made it in for Sunday lunch. Chris wished he were sitting in one too, with a plate of pub food.

'I spy some seats,' Chris said. They walked to a table at the back and sat down. Two young chaps Chris recognised were already sitting there. They eyed Rachel as she sat down. Chris eyed them and they turned back to their food. Rachel looked at her piled plate.

'Where to start,' she said. 'Where to start.'

'I usually dive in the middle and work my way outward.'

'I think I'll work from the outside in. The food gets cold first on the outside you know.'

'I know. I just do things differently.'

'Maybe we'll find that out later,' Rachel said. The two young chaps looked at her. Chris carried on eating.

When they'd finished they agreed they didn't have enough room for dessert. Chris felt bloated and horny. He sat back in his chair and looked at Rachel. He'd have to wait an hour for his stomach to settle before trying anything exerting with her.

'Let's go to my room for coffee,' he said. He gathered up Rachel's tray – she'd eaten everything – and took them to the kitchen door where there was a table with a slop bucket. He put their plates on a stack already there, and the cutlery into a bowl of soapy water. Then he walked over to the doors where Rachel was waiting.

'Let's get you signed in,' he said.

Rachel patted her stomach. 'I can hardly move.'

There was someone at reception now, a young lad who had only said ten words to Chris since he'd been there. Chris supposed that to get a job in a YMCA you had to have some strong religious beliefs; when he'd been interviewed for a room two months earlier, the manager had asked him if he went to church. Chris had said no, and thought he might've blown it, but they let him in anyway. He was sure hardly any of the residents were religious but the staff gave the impression they were. Well, if that was how miserable it made you, they could keep it.

They walked down the white-painted corridor and Rachel pointed at pieces of plaster lying on the brown carpet.

'What's been happening here?' she asked.

'It's the idiots that live here,' Chris said. 'They have fights in the corridors and throw things at each other. The walls have been getting more and more chipped since I've been here. Look behind this door. They come running down the corridor and slam the door against the wall. The handle just makes this hole bigger.'

'Why do they do it?'

'Because they're bored stiff. All the young blokes here are apprentices who work for the Ministry of Defence. They don't earn much. Most of them come from the north or Scotland. They get homesick, don't have the money to get drunk, so they stay in and destroy the place.'

'Doesn't it drive you mad?'

'It does, but what can I do? I tell some of them off now and then, but it doesn't do any good. They just swear at you and carry on.'

'You should move out.'

'I will one day. I won't be here forever.' Chris wondered if he believed that.

They came to his room and he followed Rachel in.

'Well, this is all right,' Rachel said, eyeing the place up. 'No plaster falling off the walls here.'

'When I bang my head against the walls nothing falls off. I've got a blunt head.'

'At least you've got a bed.'

'That's why I invited you back.'

Rachel smiled. She sat in the only armchair while Chris made some coffee. He dropped a Lyle Lovett tape into his cassette-radio. Rachel was wearing jeans, a rare sight. In his fantasies about her, she'd always be wearing one of her short denim skirts, and now here she was in jeans. Chris couldn't really believe that in the next few hours that fantasy would be coming true – except for the part about the skirt.

He made the coffee and handed a cup to Rachel.

'Do you have all your belongings in this room?' she asked.

Chris nodded. 'All my clothes are in that wardrobe behind you, plus a few in these drawers here. That's all I have. Plus my portable TV, my cassette-radio, and a few tapes.'

'I thought you'd have a lot of records from your disco days.'

'They were all nicked with my equipment,' Chris said.

'You've got about the same amount of stuff as me, but I'm only seventeen. I dread to think of all the things I'll accumulate by the time I'm your age.'

'People accumulate things they don't need. Most of it's attached to sentiment. They get too attached to things and can't throw them away. I throw things out regularly and keep it at a manageable level. Plus I'm not settled. If you're moving rooms all the time, you don't want stuff to take with you. When I was running my disco I had a load of stuff to haul around. All the records and equipment. In some ways, when it was nicked, I felt a sense of relief. It was a load taken off my mind.'

'Didn't you feel angry at the waste of it? It must have cost you a lot of money putting it all together.'

'I did at first but that soon passed. Actually, it seemed to wake me up.'

'How do you mean?'

'I was in a rut, sick of being a travelling disco and of being on the dole at the same time. But I didn't have the guts to stop myself doing it. Then I was forced to, and forced to think again. It woke me up, got my brain working. Sometimes you need that. That's why some people, after a personal tragedy, pick themselves up and go on to better things. It gives them a kick up the ass. Unfortunately, the off-licence is hardly a better thing, although I thought it was at the time.'

'I'd prefer not to have the tragedy.'

'So would most people. But most times you have no say in the matter.'

'No. Is there a toilet near here?'

'Down the corridor to the right.'

'I'll be back in a minute.'

Chris looked out the window while Rachel was gone. It was a dull day outside, a grey day best suited for staying indoors. From where he sat he could see the rear YMCA car park and several residents working on their cars. It obviously wasn't too grey for them.

When Rachel came back, she shut the door and walked over to him. She stood between his legs and they kissed.

'Do you want to go as well?' she asked.

Chris shook his head.

'Has your stomach settled?' he asked.

Rachel nodded.

'Well what are we waiting for?'

They kissed a while longer and then started on each others jeans. Rachel unzipped Chris while he struggled with her buttoned ones. He had just got the last one undone when there was a loud knock on the door.

'Anyone in?'

Chris stopped his hand and started doing Rachel up again.

'Can't we pretend we're not in?' she whispered.

'It's the police. I recognise the voice. Just a minute!' he called out.

He zipped himself up and pulled his pullover down. He waited for Rachel to finish and then opened the door for Detective Sergeant Morgan.

'Sorry to bother you on a Sunday,' Morgan said coming in. Then he saw Rachel. 'Oh, doubly sorry. I didn't think you'd have company.'

'Why? You think no one likes me?'

'No, no. I just didn't think. I was passing anyway, so I thought I'd drop in. Let you know the latest news.'

'I can turn on the TV for that.' Chris didn't shut the door hoping it would hurry Morgan up. He introduced Rachel. Now Morgan was standing there saying nothing. He was listening to the Lyle Lovett cassette.

'You're a country fan?' he asked.

'For a long time,' Chris said.

'Me too. I like Crystal Gayle myself,' Morgan said. 'Lovely voice, lovely hair. Saw her at The Palladium once.'

'I'll see what I can do next time,' Chris said. Rachel looked at him.

'I've just had another of your free meals,' Morgan said. 'You get good food here.'

Chris tried to hurry him along. 'So what's the latest news?'

'May I?' Morgan said, and then sat down in the armchair. Chris thought he may as well close the door. Rachel sat on the bed, so Chris was left standing. He leaned on his desk, looked down at Morgan, and waited.

'There was another mugging last night. The same place as yours, almost exactly the same time, but this time with a worse result.'

Now Chris was interested. 'You mean they got away with it?'

Morgan nodded. 'A couple of girls from one of the clothes shops. They had two night wallets with them. They'd had a busy day so they'd put the cash in one and the cheques and credit cards in another. The mugger got away with the one full of cash.'

'That's bad luck. Was anyone hurt?'

'No. The girls were shaken. They were both shoved around a bit. But he didn't hit either of them.'

'Did anyone see him?'

'He was too quick for the girls to see much of him. An old lady did though. She was walking up the road towards the Shopping Mall. She saw the man come out from behind the bank and walk towards the girls. She was walking right behind him. Then when he turned with the money and was running back towards her she took a swipe at him with her handbag.'

'Did she get him?'

'Right across the face. It threw him off stride a little, but he carried on running and jumped over the same wall yours did. The lady heard a car starting on the other side, so he must've driven or been driven away.'

'So she got a good look at him?'

'We've got a description which is similar to yours, except for one thing.'

Chris waited. The tape clicked off.

'He was wearing a woollen hat but the lady thought she saw blonde hair poking out from underneath. She thinks he was blonde.'

'Well, that's a pity.'

'I thought it was quite promising really.'

'Why?' But Chris knew what was coming as soon as he'd asked.

'Wasn't the friend of the bloke who mugged you blonde? Or the bloke you think mugged you, I should say. Can't accuse people just yet.' Morgan smiled at Rachel.

'You think they're part of a team? They're taking turns mugging people?'

'It could be. Sounds feasible.'

'Have you done one of those drawings from the lady's description? Maybe I could have a look at it.'

'No. She didn't get that good a look.'

'So we're back to square one.'

'I just wanted to see what you thought of my theory.'

'On a Sunday.'

'And ask you to keep your eyes open. If you see either of these chaps again I want you to let me know. I'll give you a phone number.' Morgan got out his wallet and took out a business card. 'That's the station number. Leave a message for me if I'm not there. I probably won't be.'

'How about your home number as well?'

'I only go there to sleep. When I sleep I don't want interruptions.'

'Okay.'

'How's the old lady?' Rachel asked.

'Fine. She thought it was good fun.'

'She must have a lot of guts.'

'Either that or else she's stupid. We prefer people not to get involved in situations like these.' Morgan studied Chris. 'Your face looks pretty normal again. Have you had any compensation from work, yet?'

'I'm going to get some money for damaged clothes. About seventy quid I hope.'

'That's not too bad. Have you thought of applying to the Criminal Injuries Compensation Board?'

'What's that?'

'It's a place where you get compensated for violent crimes. It's in London. I don't know the address off the top of my head. Ask at a police station and they'll give it to you. Then write and ask for a form.'

'Then what happens?'

'You fill in the form telling how and when you got hit. Then about two years later you'll get compensated. The minimum amount they deal with is four hundred pounds. You'll get that at least.'

'Sounds good.'

'Be sure to apply soon though, so that your injury is officially logged. It's too late if you apply in a year, say, when you've developed a nasty twitch from the injuries. They'll say you could've got the twitch from something else.'

'But I won't get a twitch.'

'Maybe not, but you want your injury on record, like I said, in case complications set in later. It could be a twitch, it could be a haemorrhage.'

'Okay, I'll look into it. I wish you'd told me before.'

'I'm not a Citizens Advice Bureau. Your company should've told you about it.'

'Shows how much they care.' Chris looked at the floor and felt cheered by the thought of a free four hundred pounds. Maybe he'd try and get mugged again some day.

'How much money did the mugger get away with?' Rachel asked.

'Just over three thousand,' Morgan said. 'A nice little sum if there's only two of you.'

'Or if there's only one of you,' Rachel said.

Morgan nodded. 'Well, I must be going. Sorry to bother you again. I thought you'd be interested to know.' He stood up.

'I was,' Chris said. He opened the door. Now Morgan was chuckling at him.

'I went to the scene of the crime this morning, you know. Just to see if there was anything unusual in the cold light of day. Well, just next to the Portakabin at the back of the bank, I found a pile of human excrement. I presume you've eaten already?' Morgan turned to Rachel who nodded.

'It seems our criminal had to relieve himself just before he went through with it.'

'Nice.'

'Because there are no toilet facilities there he used part of an old cement packet as toilet paper.'

Rachel was turning her nose up at this. Chris wished Morgan would leave. Now Morgan was grinning widely.

'So all we have to do,' he said, 'is find someone walking around town with a stiff behind.' Morgan shook his head. 'I've never seen anything like it.'

Rachel started laughing then and Chris found himself smiling too. Morgan walked into the hallway laughing. 'Just watch the way people walk,' he said. 'Watch the way they walk.'

Chris closed the door and looked at Rachel. She was still laughing.

'Now where were we?' he said.

Sixteen

Dashy thought of the obvious on Sunday, while he was watching live football on TV – and wondered why he hadn't thought of it before. He picked up the telephone book from the sideboard and found Kevin's address in there. Under Jenkins. Just where it would be, considering that was his name.

On Monday morning, Dashy took the bus to see Kevin. He wanted to catch him before he went out, so nine o'clock seemed early enough. He sat on the bottom deck as the bus trundled down the Blackfen road. Then he saw Kevin's estate with the distinctive red brick of every house. He pressed the bell, and got off at the next stop.

Walking along the street, Dashy tried to arrange the thoughts in his head, working out exactly what he'd say to Kevin. Basically, he was going to ask Kevin for some of the money from the mugging because he felt he deserved it. If it hadn't been for his failed attempt on Chris, then Kevin wouldn't have had the idea of trying it himself in the first place. Therefore, as original mastermind, didn't he have a right to some of the money? With his share he could pay Chris to keep his mouth shut. He wouldn't tell Kevin about that part. It would be tricky to handle because he sensed that Kevin's friendship wasn't going to last much longer. The way Kevin treated him like shit, avoiding him most days, getting away quickly when they did meet, told Dashy that Kevin had tired of his company. He didn't know why after all the good times they'd had in the bookies, but if that was the way he wanted it, it was no skin off his nose.

Dashy walked on to the estate and looked for number one. It was right at the start, of course. Then Dashy remembered that Kevin's old man had bought the original show house, the one already fitted with furniture, curtains, and false books, the one potential buyers tramped around when they were looking for a two-bedroomed house. Dashy wouldn't like a house that hundreds of people had already walked through, but he supposed it saved a lot of decorating. He walked up the short front path, the neatly-trimmed lawn on either side, and rang the front doorbell. The door was opened by Kevin's father.

'Is Kevin up yet?' Dashy asked.

'It'll be a miracle if he is,' his father said. 'Wait there and I'll have a look. Who are you?'

'My name's Leo. Just tell him Dashy.' The father went upstairs and left Dashy outside. Leo. He used his real name so little nowadays, it felt uncomfortable when he said it. Maybe he should start using it more often. That was one thing he'd liked about Chris when he'd been in the pub with him the other night. He'd wanted to call him Leo straight away, had dismissed Dashy as a stupid name. Dashy thought it was stupid as well. Hell, he was twenty-five, maybe it was about time he stopped using his nickname and became a grown-up. Maybe with a change of name, his luck would change. He heard voices from inside and then a tired looking Kevin walked down the stairs in a worn light blue towelling bathrobe. He had a freshly-lit cigarette in his mouth. He came to the door and said, 'What's up?'

Dashy didn't like the way he said that. As if he didn't want to see him again. 'Can I see you a minute?' he asked.

'What about? I'm not even awake yet.'

'I can't tell you here. Let me in, will you?'

Kevin didn't say anything, just pushed the door open with his foot and waved Dashy in. Like getting to see the queen, Dashy thought.

'Upstairs,' Kevin said.

Dashy followed him up the steep narrow staircase. They came to a small landing and went into Kevin's room. Dashy had never been in one of these Wimpy homes before and he was shocked at how small and unreal it looked. He was used to his parents old, homely place, and this house just looked too new, too perfect. That is, until he entered Kevin's room. It was a mess. Kevin's bed was a low foldaway type with blankets untidily thrown back. There was no wardrobe, so Kevin's clothes were lying in piles on the floor. If the house came furnished, then how come this room wasn't? A foldaway chair sat by the bed with a bedside lamp on it. Three paperbacks were scattered on the floor, all with war covers. Dashy had never read a book in his life. There were also a few magazines strewn around, one of them a *Men Only*. There was nowhere for Dashy to sit, so he leaned on the window-ledge while Kevin sat on the bed. Kevin pulled an overflowing ashtray towards him and flicked his cigarette at it. The ash missed and landed on the carpet.

'What time is it?' Kevin asked.

'Nine-thirty.'

'Stone me. Too early for a Monday.'

'I thought you'd be up by now.'

'Well, I am now. What did you want?'

Dashy looked at Kevin and decided to get it out quickly. 'I came to see how much money you got on Saturday night.' Kevin looked up sharply at him. 'And I want my share of it.'

'What the fuck're you talking about?'

'I saw you on Saturday night. First off, I saw you getting into your Cortina, and secondly, I saw you drive away from behind the bank. I know what you did, so there's no point denying it.'

'Have you been following me?'

'I followed you out of BHS on Saturday. You were acting so odd, I thought I'd see what was up. I saw you driving out of the car park in a light blue Cortina. God knows where you got that from, I don't want to know. I put two and two together and figured you might be doing a mugging that night. I went behind the bank just after five and saw the Cortina. I was standing there when you came over the wall. I saw the night wallet roll under the car. I saw you looking for it.'

'Well, fuck me. Aren't you the little Columbo.' A grin came on Kevin's face. 'That was a sticky moment there. I couldn't work out where the wallet had gone. I was thinking, all that work for nothing, it's gone and rolled down a drain!'

'I felt like shouting out to you. I knew where it was.'

'Why didn't you?'

'You would've shitted yourself. You were panicking as it was.'

'Well, so would you have been. I've never pulled anything like that before. Where were you hiding, anyway?'

'Right opposite the car. In between some garages.'

'You bastard!'

It was almost like old times again, but Dashy wasn't convinced. Kevin could just as soon revert to his off-hand mood.

'So, now you want some of the money, because you've got something on me?' Kevin said.

'If it wasn't for me, you wouldn't have done it in the first place. I gave you the idea.'

'I was going to tell you about it, anyway. I just wanted to keep it a secret until it was done. To tell you the truth, I didn't trust you. I thought you'd blab about it to Helen, or someone.'

'I wouldn't.'

'It was safer like this. The less people that knew the better. You didn't have to know anyway.'

'So how much did you get?'

'One and a half grand. There was a load of cheques and credit cards in it. I threw them away.'

'Shit. That's all right, though. One and a half grand. How much do I get?'

'Five hundred for the idea and to keep your mouth shut. If I give you that much you'll have to keep quiet because if I get caught, I'll tell them you've got part of it too.'

'Thanks for being so trusting.'

'I've never trusted anyone in my life, and I'm not about to start.'

Dashy watched Kevin stub out his cigarette. He couldn't believe it had been that easy! Five hundred quid was more than he'd hoped for. He could give half of that to Chris and he'd be clear. He was sure that would be enough. Chris didn't strike him as the greedy type.

'So when can I have it?' he asked.

'Now, if you like. Go downstairs and make me a cup of coffee. Talk to my dad for five minutes and make sure he doesn't come up. I've hidden it in the back of his wardrobe, so I'll have to get it out of there.'

'Okay. Five minutes.'

Dashy went downstairs with an excited feeling in his stomach. In a few minutes time, he'd be walking out with a nice wad of money, and his problems would be over. He went into the kitchen and found Kevin's dad washing up. He turned from the sink and said hello.

'I've come to make Kevin a cup of coffee. Can I put on the kettle?'

'Are you his nursemaid?'

'No, I'm having one, too.'

'You'll have to fill it up. I've just emptied it.'

Dashy picked up the kettle and leaned awkwardly across

Mr Jenkins to reach the tap. He could smell the BO on the grey post office uniform. He plugged the kettle in and thought desperately for something to say. The washing-up would keep the old man busy for five minutes but he had to make sure.

'Have they got any Christmas vacancies at the Post Office?' he asked.

Mr Jenkins looked up. 'If you apply now you may get something. I've been trying to get Kevin to work there.'

'Yeah? I'd be very interested.'

When Dashy left the house fifteen minutes later, not only did he have five hundred pounds in his anorak pocket, but also the name of someone to ring at the post office. As he walked to the bus stop, he was thinking that maybe his luck was really about to change.

*

Chris turned at the sound of Ron's voice calling him to the telephone. He put down the duster he was holding and walked towards the office. He never got calls at work, so he couldn't think who it could be. He picked up the phone and looked down at Ron at his desk. The bastard would stay there to see who it was.

'Hello?'

'Chris?'

'Yeah.'

'It's Leo.'

'Oh, hello.' Ron looked up at the change in Chris's voice. 'What can I do for you?'

'Can we meet sometime? I've got something for you. You said you wanted something in return?'

'Yeah.'

'Well, I've got something.'

'Like what?'

'Like money.'

'That sounds promising.'

'So where do you want to meet?'

'You name a place.'

'You don't sound too enthusiastic.'

'I am. Very.' Chris wished Leo would get on with it. He could hardly say a word with Ron sitting there.

'I think we should avoid anywhere public,' Leo said. 'How about the car park in the Shopping Mall.'

'Okay. Whereabouts?'

'On the first level. By the wall that looks over the High Street. When do you get off?'

'Six o'clock. Let's make it five-past.'

'Okay. See you then.'

Chris hung up and Ron looked up at him. 'Old friend?' he asked.

'What the fuck's it got to do with you?' Chris said, and walked back into the shop.

*

Chris could honestly say that he'd never been up to the Shopping Mall car park before. Why should he? He didn't have a car and he'd never been shopping in the Mall with someone who could drive. It was no big loss. See one car park and you've seen them all.

He got out of the elevator and walked across the tarmac to the far wall. He looked around for Leo and saw him leaning against the wall, his back to the street below.

'Why all the secrecy?' Chris asked when he'd reached him.

Without saying a word, Leo reached into his pocket and brought out a wad of notes. He handed them to Chris.

'What's this?'

'Two hundred and fifty quid.'

Chris reached out for it. 'Thanks. Where did you get it from?'

'It doesn't matter. You said you wanted something in return for what I did, so here it is. You don't want more do you? I thought that would be enough.'

'No. This is fine.' Chris put it in his jacket pocket.

'So it's all over now. I've got your assurance you won't tell the police about me?'

'You've got my assurance.'

'You don't know how relieved I feel. I've been feeling bad for two weeks.'

'Well, you shouldn't have done it in the first place.'

'No. I've been regretting it ever since.'

'Well. Thanks a lot.' Chris held out his hand to Leo and they shook. 'Next time remember to hold back your punch a little. I've still got a stiff face.'

'I'm sorry. If I'd of known you then, I wouldn't of done it.'

'Well, it's done.' Chris looked over Dashy's shoulder and

into the street below. 'You know this is a perfect view of the nightsafe. Is this where you cased me out from?'

'No. I only found this place afterwards. I did it all from down there in the café.'

'That's what I thought. You know there was another mugging on Saturday. Almost exactly the same as yours. The bloke got away with three grand.'

'Three grand!'

'Yeah. A nice little haul.'

'Jesus Christ!'

'What's up?'

Chris could see Leo squirming on the spot. He was pretty sure the money in his pocket was part of Saturday's mugging. He could almost see Leo thinking, wondering whether to tell him about it or not.

'Tell me,' he said.

Leo stalled another few seconds before he spoke.

'I know who did the mugging. It was my friend Kevin. Or ex-friend as he's rapidly becoming. I saw him this morning and asked for a cut seeing as how it was my idea originally. He told me he'd got one and a half grand.'

Chris grinned. 'He's lying then. I got the amount from the police.'

'Why should they tell you?'

'They're keeping me in touch. They thought maybe it was you again, except that the bloke had blonde hair. They think the two of you are working as a team, doing alternate muggings.'

'Jesus!'

'You'd better stay clear of Kevin until the whole thing blows over.'

'Yeah, but he's sitting on two and a half grand.'

'Well, he's conned you out of it. There's nothing you can do about it.'

'I could go back and ask for more.'

'He'd just deny it.'

'I could threaten him.'

'With what?'

Leo had to think about that one. 'The bastard doesn't scare easy. I could threaten to beat him up but I'm not sure if I could manage it. He used to be a truck driver. He's as strong as an ox. You've seen him anyway. You know how tough he looks.'

'I wouldn't fancy tangling with him. If he's a truck driver, how come he's on the dole? There's always a lot of work for HGV drivers.'

'He's been banned for a year. Drinking and driving.'

'Oh.'

'He's just killing time until he gets his licence back. He did the mugging because he was bored. And to show me up.'

'But the police told me he used a car to drive away from the mugging.'

'That's right. I saw him.'

Now Chris was getting interested. 'How come?'

'I followed him. He was acting suspicious so I thought maybe he was going to pull something. I went behind the bank, saw his getaway car, and waited for him to come over the wall.'

'You saw him coming over the wall and driving away?'

'It was quite funny. As he was climbing over he dropped the wallet and it rolled under the car. It took him ages to find it. He was down on his hands and knees, shitting himself.'

'He couldn't of been. He'd already done that.'

'What do you mean?'

'While he was waiting on the other side he went for a crap. The police found a pile of shit there the next morning.'

'Yeah?'

'And the funny thing is, he didn't have anything to wipe his ass with. So he used a bit of cement wrapper that was lying there. The cops're now looking for someone with a stiff ass.'

'Ha! I wish I'd been there to see that.'

'The sort of thing you'd like to get on film. Bribe him with it.'

'That's what we need. Something to hang on him.'

They fell into silence. Chris looked down at the street and wondered what he was getting himself into. It was an interesting situation. If he played his cards right he could come out of this with a fair bit of money. There was two and a half grand sitting with this Kevin bloke and he wanted some of it. A couple of grand would be nice. He needed a lever on Kevin though, but he couldn't think of one at the moment.

'Let's go,' he said to Leo. 'We'll have to think this through. Try and think of something we can get him on. It's not enough you saw him drive away. You could threaten him, but then he could threaten you about your mugging. You both know too

much about each other. You cancel each other out. I think I'll
have to be the one that threatens him. And we'll have to be
quick about it. He may be thinking of leaving. Going on a
cruise or something.'

They walked across the tarmac towards the lift.

'So how much did he give you altogether?' Chris asked.

'Five hundred.'

'That's not bad out of one and a half grand. You must've
thought he was being generous.'

'I thought it was a bit too easy. I thought he'd be reluctant to
give me anything.'

'He must be smirking into his socks right now. Feeling pretty pleased with himself.'

'We'll have to think of something. I'd hate to see him getting
away with that much dough.'

'We'll think of something,' Chris said, but he didn't feel as
confident as he sounded.

Seventeen

Tuesday, November 22nd.

It would soon be December and that was what Eunice called her Three-D time. December – Depression – Drink.

Eunice hated Christmas, dreaded its coming every year. Christmas was a time for children and families, and if you were single you automatically felt cut off, alone in a world having a few days of fun while you were alone having a few days of drink. Hard drink. She hoped her worries would have lifted a little by then, and give her a chance of making it through in one piece.

She leaned into the pump on the bar at The Coach and Horses and pulled the first pint of the day. She was thinking of volunteering her services over the Christmas break to help take her mind off things. Then there would only be Christmas Day to get through on her own.

Eunice had spent the previous Christmas in the flat of a pilot called John whom she'd met just two weeks before. They'd struck up a conversation in The Bricklayers Arms one evening, and had slept with each other just two days later. It was a short relationship that barely lasted a week into the New Year. But it was short and sweet for them both; both had been dreading the days drawing in, and with the help of each others company, had made it through the 'festive season' as painlessly as they could. Eunice wished she could find someone like that again.

She plonked the pint in front of her first customer and thought of the weekend she'd just been through…

After deciding not to go to work on Saturday, she had walked into the village to her local video shop and rented a copy of *Roxanne*. Opening another bottle of German white, her third of the day, she had sat in her darkened sitting-room and let the film cheer her up. She had wondered if some day she'd meet a man like Steve Martin, someone who would write her romantic letters and then woo her from underneath a balcony. With that hopeful thought in her head, she had dropped off to sleep.

When she'd woken up, it was dark outside and the blank TV screen was glaring in front of her. The video clock said 6.32.

Eunice turned the TV off with the remote control and sat on the back of the sofa looking down at the yard below. She watched some of the other residents return home with bags of food and drink. She envied them their settled lives and began to feel depressed again. But she was shocked out of this mood when she saw her car turning off the road and into the driveway. She watched as it slowly disappeared around the corner towards the garages. She wasn't able to see who the driver was.

A few minutes later she saw Kevin come around the building and walk up the path to the flats' entrance. Feeling scared, she rushed off the sofa to the front door and made sure it was locked. She stood in the dark hallway and heard footsteps climbing the wooden stairs. The footsteps advanced along the brick hall and stopped outside her door. She braced herself for the sound of the doorbell, and stood back in terror, just as the letterbox was pushed open. A white envelope sailed through and landed on the floor with a clink. Then Kevin's footsteps retreated down the stairs towards the front door.

Eunice went back to the sitting-room window and looked out. She watched Kevin walk to the road and head for the bus stop. Only when he was completely out of sight did she return to the front door and pick up the envelope. Inside were her car keys.

She took the envelope to the kitchen, turned on the light, and sat down. Written on the envelope, in a childlike scrawl were the words: *Sorry. I took these by mistake. Hope you didn't miss them. See you around. K.* Eunice sat looking at the envelope not knowing what to think. Did Kevin think she was dumb? She tried to think what he'd been up to.

Okay. He'd taken her car keys on Friday because he needed the car for something on Saturday. He finishes with the car and pops the keys back through the door, thinking that either she hasn't noticed, or hasn't got a spare set of keys to check inside the garage. He was right about that. But figuring she wouldn't notice the missing keys? Wasn't that taking it a bit far?

Eunice felt anger welling up inside her. Just as she was getting over the bedroom incident, the guy intruded again and made her life a misery. She didn't like the way he'd ended the letter with *See you around* either. Was he going to come into the pub again? It was the sort of thing a bloke like that would do. If he did, she'd grab the nearest bottle to hand and throw it at his head. It would be worth getting the sack for.

Eunice hadn't been to work on the Sunday either, and had spent half the day drunk, kicking off at midday, before snapping out of it in the evening, realising she was acting like a fool. She'd taken a hot shower at eight o'clock, trying to steam the drink out of her system, and had made a big plate of pasta with meat sauce, hoping a good stomach-bolster would be good for the mind, too. She'd been right. On Monday she'd woken up feeling pleasantly drowsy and ready to take on the world again. She'd gone to work as normal.

By Tuesday, although she felt strong enough to handle Kevin if he walked through the saloon bar door, Eunice still felt her nerves stand on end every time the door swung open. She would look up from what she was doing, and breathe a sigh of relief when she saw it wasn't him. With each passing hour the threat became less and less, but she was still convinced that Kevin would walk through there one day soon. She hoped that by the time he did, she'd be ready for him.

*

Chris was sitting with Amanda in the BHS cafeteria. The place was crowded with families starting to do their Christmas shopping. Chris chewed on a sandwich without enthusiasm and looked at Amanda.

'How did you manage to wangle a day off work?' he asked her.

'We're not very busy,' Amanda said, 'and everyone else takes days off to do Christmas shopping. I thought I'd take advantage of it although I don't have that much to do. Are we going to buy each other presents this year?'

'Well, I'm going to buy you something.' He saw a smile come on Amanda's face.

'Good. I've already bought yours.'

'Just as well I said that.'

'Where are you spending Christmas?' Amanda asked. This would be their first one apart for two years. Chris was dreading it but knew they shouldn't spend it together for old times sake.

'Well, the YMCA shuts for Christmas would you believe, so I'm really in trouble.'

'They throw everyone out?'

Chris nodded. 'Because most of the residents are apprentices they've all got homes to go to. They'll be away for two weeks or so. That leaves about ten of us normal citizens and they're not going to keep on a full quota of staff just for us. The place shuts Christmas Day and Boxing Day and I won't even be able to get in. I'll be able to sleep there after that though.'

'That's terrible. You can always stay with us if you like.'

'I'll bear that in mind, but I really think we should spend it apart,' he said.

'Well, don't force yourself.' Amanda's eyes started to look tearful. Chris wanted to comfort her in some way, but didn't like to do anything in this crowded place.

'You know, at the YMCA they have a Christmas dinner a few days before everyone leaves?,' he said. 'They put table-cloths on all the tables and you're allowed to bring in a bottle of wine. That's a bit of a breakthrough because drink is officially banned from the place.'

'Are you going to go?'

'No. I'll avoid it like the plague.'

'We've got a Christmas dinner too. That'll be in a restaurant though.'

'Here we are thinking about Christmas and it's over a month away.'

'It seems to rule everyone's thoughts from November onwards. I thought I was different.'

'You are different. You're thinking about it because you dread it. The same as me.'

Amanda nodded. Chris looked at people queueing at the self-service. Stuffing themselves with cakes and buns. Trying to keep their tearaway kids in sight. 'Let's get out of here,' he said. They stood up and left.

Amanda walked with Chris back to the off-licence. They stood outside the front window and Amanda looked at the display, and then noticed Rachel on the other side at the till.

'How's Rachel?' she asked.

'She's fine,' Chris said, trying to sound non-committal.

'She looks different. I like her hair. She's growing up quickly.'

'I don't notice. I see her nearly every day.'

'Come on! She's quite attractive really. I never used to think she was.'

'Why don't you go in and tell her?'

'No. I've got to go.'

They gave each other a kiss and Chris walked into the shop. He smiled at Rachel. They'd been smiling at each other a lot since Sunday. After their interruption by Morgan they'd spent the whole afternoon in bed until Rachel had left around seven o'clock. Chris was already looking forward to the next time. The weekend would be the earliest opportunity, though.

'Someone called for you while you were out,' Rachel said to him now. 'He left a number and wants you to ring him back. He said it's urgent.' She handed him a piece of paper. Chris looked at the number and didn't recognise it. He guessed it would be Leo.

'Can you delay your lunch for five minutes?' Chris asked.

'No,' Rachel said, smiling and shaking her head.

Chris went to the office and found Ron in there. He walked straight back out to the till telephone.

'There's no privacy in this world,' he said.

'I'll promise not to eavesdrop.'

Chris looked at Rachel as he dialled the number, her nice little body in a short, black, corduroy skirt. Bare legs as usual. He could walk right behind her and lift it up. Try something without the customers noticing. He heard Leo answer at the other end.

'You had some urgent news for me,' Chris said.

'Well, not urgent exactly, but just a thought.'

'Tell me.'

'I've been thinking about the car that Kevin used. The light blue Cortina?'

'Yeah.'

'Well, I don't reckon he stole it, because he wouldn't have the brains or balls to do that. Plus you have to know how to wire one, and he certainly wouldn't know how to do that. So I reckon he must've borrowed it from someone.'

'His father?'

'No. I was round at his house the other day when I picked up my money and I didn't see it there. In fact there was a Toyota parked in the driveway. That must've been his dads.'

'I wouldn't know a Toyota if you thrust one in front of me. So where did he get it from?'

'The only other person I can think of is this woman he's

been knocking off. An older woman. He's been seeing her for a couple of weeks. She's called Eunice and she works in The Coach and Horses in Blackfen. You know it?'

'I've been there once. What does she look like?'

Rachel turned to look at him.

'Well, he said she was older, so I suspect she's somewhere in her forties or fifties. And she had dyed blonde hair and a great body. He told me after the first time he bonked her how great she was in the sack. Told me just about everything they did. She sounds like the kind of woman I'd like to meet.'

'So she works behind the bar when? In the evenings or during the day?'

'Well, he used to meet her during the day, but I think she works evenings as well.'

'Sounds promising. Look, I'll go there tonight and see if I can have a few words with her. I'll give you a ring tomorrow. This is your home number, isn't it?'

'Yeah. I'll be waiting.'

Chris hung up and looked at Rachel. She had a funny look on her face.

'You're going to see another woman tonight?' she said. 'I thought we were going out.'

'Something's come up. I'll have to go to this other pub. Sorry.'

'As long as something else doesn't come up,' she teased.

Chris walked behind her and grabbed her by the waist. 'If you keep standing like that something will.'

'Don't let me stop you,' Rachel laughed. Then they had to act serious because an old woman walked up and placed a bottle of sherry in front of them. Chris jabbed Rachel softly in the ribs and walked away.

*

Eunice didn't really like the early evening crowd at The Coach and Horses – it was mostly businessmen and young people from offices.

She found the businessmen the worst to deal with. They thought they were hot shots in their suits, some of them smoking foul-smelling cigars and trying to joke with her as they ordered, making smutty comments as she pulled the pumps. She didn't like the way they drank either, a lot of 'shorts' that made their breath smell even worse. She was glad she wasn't a

wife waiting at home for one of them to return to the supper
table. Breathe smoke and whisky all over her. But hadn't she
been that with Michael? In many ways she was glad to be single.

The young people from the offices were nearly as bad. Many
of them were working in their first job, and the combination of
wage packets and sex brought out the worst in them. They
were loud, crude, drank too much, and flirted too much.
Eunice dreaded to think of all the affairs that either started or
ended in the pub. But then again, isn't that where most of hers
started? Yes, but she liked to think hers were a bit more romantic. If you discounted Kevin of course. That had just been lust
that had gone wrong.

Once the office people drifted out, the pub would get quiet,
and then start to busy up again as the evening crowd arrived.
These were the locals, people she knew better and who were
more friendly. The last part of the evening was the best time, as
things started to liven up, and people for the most part went
home happy. Eunice would have two half-pints of lager during
the evening and leave it at that – and she wouldn't have to pay
either. She had more offers of drinks than she could accept.
She'd accepted the first one that night from someone she hadn't
seen before. A chap who looked to be in his late twenties, and
nice looking. He stayed at the bar, catching her eye from time to
time and smiling. He'd given her a nice smile when he'd
ordered his pint. Eunice knew he would start talking to her
soon. She knew the type straight away.

*

Chris had given Rachel a goodnight kiss outside the shop,
and had then waited half an hour for a bus to Blackfen. The
ride only took fifteen minutes and he got off as near The Coach
and Horses as possible.

The pub was on the main road at a crossroads. The one time
Chris had been there was for a jazz evening about a year before
with Amanda. Neither of them liked jazz particularly, but it
had seemed a good idea at the time, somewhere to go for an
evening out. But when the evening had ended they'd still not
particularly liked jazz.

Chris pushed open the door to the public bar and looked for
a barmaid who matched Leo's description of Eunice. There was
only a young chap who looked very busy. He walked into the

saloon bar and there the barmaid exactly fitted the description. He walked straight out and went to look in the car park behind the pub. There was the light blue Cortina. He went back into the bar and ordered a pint of lager for himself and bought Eunice a half.

Now that he'd established that Eunice was the provider of Kevin's getaway car, Chris had to find some way of bringing the subject up with her. For all he knew, she might be in on the whole thing. She could've lent the car to Kevin in exchange for some of the money. Somehow he doubted that though, because Kevin hadn't been seeing her for long. No, Kevin must've borrowed it while she was out.

Chris emptied his glass and motioned Eunice over for another one. She took his glass and pulled the pump in front of him.

'Is your name Eunice?' he asked her.

She looked up surprised. 'Yes. How do you know?'

'I was told you work here by someone called Kevin Jenkins.'

At the mention of that name Eunice's arm froze on the pump but she composed herself quickly and carried on pulling. Chris noticed a defensive look on her face.

'If you're a friend of his, you're no friend of mine,' Eunice said, placing the pint in front of him.

Chris took his time counting his loose change. He'd stumbled on a touchy subject. 'He's no friend of mine either,' he said. 'If anything he's the opposite.'

'We've got something in common then. The less I see of him the better. You can tell him that if you see him.'

'I won't be seeing him socially.'

'You know him though?'

'Not really. I'm trying to find out about him. I'm trying to find out how he got hold of a light blue Cortina last Saturday.'

'My Cortina?'

'That's what I thought.' Chris gave Eunice the money.

'You're not a policeman are you? You don't look like one.'

Chris laughed. 'No.'

'Can you meet me when I get off?' she said. 'Maybe we're on the same side after all.'

'What time?'

'I should get away by eleven-thirty. Wait for me in the car park. By my car.'

'Okay.'

Chris watched as Eunice served someone else. He couldn't help looking at her behind. He always seemed to have sex on his mind these days. He looked at his watch. It was only half past seven. What the hell could he do until eleven-thirty?

Eighteen

Kevin was getting restless staying at home and was wondering whether it was time to move on. He had two and a half grand to spend, no reason for staying in Blackfen, and still another five months to go until he could get his licence back. It would be nice to go somewhere for a while.

It was Wednesday, ten in the morning, his father already at work. He sat in the darkened sitting-room watching a video of *Mad Max*. It was one of the few videos he owned, the first he had ever gone out and bought. He sat there wondering how many videos he could buy with two and a half grand. Then he worked it out. Two hundred and fifty at the most. That wasn't many at all. Or maybe he could buy a car like the one Mel Gibson had and drive off into the sunset. Except you couldn't do that kind of thing in Britain. There weren't any deserts with sunsets, just towns, hills and cities. The whole place depressed him.

Kevin had to laugh when he thought of Dashy and the way he'd gone off happy as a sandman with his five hundred quid. That had been quick thinking to send him downstairs to keep his dad at bay. Of course the money hadn't been in his old man's wardrobe, it had been right there underneath his foldaway bed! He'd had to get Dashy out of the room so he wouldn't see the whole wad when he counted off his measly five hundred. It was a pity Dashy had gone off with anything, but it wasn't such a small price to pay for his silence. He'd never have thought Dashy smart enough to figure out what he'd been up to, though. Following him to the car park – cheeky bugger – and then watching him come over the wall! The bloke was getting ideas above his station.

Kevin turned off Mel Gibson and went to the window. He looked out at the bleak weather-worn estate and scratched himself through his pyjamas. He was starting to feel horny again. Maybe he could go to The Coach and Horses and apologise to Eunice. The silly bitch wouldn't take him back though. Not that he'd want her back. Just one more screw would do. That was always the way when you split up with a woman. After a few days you started missing their bodies and wanted to fuck them even more.

The telephone rang then and shocked him out of his day-dreaming. It never rang when his father was at work, so who the hell could it be? He walked over and picked it up.

*

The first thing Chris did that morning was try and find Bill. He walked through the YMCA corridors without any luck. Bill wasn't in his room and he wasn't in the canteen. Chris tried all the toilets and eventually found him in a cubicle on the second floor. Chris was puzzled because Bill's room was on the ground floor. He stood outside the cubicle and talked through the door.

'Why do you go to the toilet on the second floor Bill?'

'Because it's quiet up here. There's less people around. I can relax my bowels in peace. But now you've found out, I suppose you'll be coming here.'

'I won't tell a soul.'

'So what do you want?'

'I need to borrow your video camera. And a tape.'

'What for? I don't lend it out to just anyone you know.'

'I just want to take some pictures of Rachel,' Chris lied. 'She wants to see herself on TV.'

'I don't hire out for porn.'

Chris laughed. 'These are innocent, fully-clothed pictures. Just pictures of her working, things like that.'

'Why not rent one?'

'It'll cost me thirty quid.'

'So you come to me to get it for free?'

'You're the original Mr Generous,' Chris said. 'Or at least, I thought you were.'

There was only silence from the other side of the door. Chris waited.

'Wait for me outside, will you?' Bill said. 'I'll be out in five minutes.'

Chris smiled and went into the corridor. He walked to the rest-room and sat in an armchair looking out of the window. He could see the main road and the bus stop. It was his day off, so he wouldn't be walking up there later.

He thought about his meeting the previous night with Eunice. She'd come out of the pub at eleven-thirty as promised, and they'd talked for twenty minutes by her car. To kill the hours waiting for her, Chris had caught a bus to Leo's, and they'd sat in his bedroom going over things, ironing out a few details in their plan. Chris had spent the first ten minutes looking at the sporting photos on Leo's walls. Leo was proud to give him a guided tour. He'd met his parents as well and they seemed a pretty close family.

Eunice had told Chris how Kevin had taken her car without permission – which was stealing in Chris's language – and how she'd seen him bring it back. She'd told him about the envelope dropped through the door with the keys in it. Chris had asked her what Kevin was wearing so he'd have something concrete to catch him on. He knew straight away that this was the lever he could use for getting most of the two and a half grand.

Chris hadn't told Eunice about the robbery or why Kevin had needed the car; he'd told her that he needed the information for some friends of his who wanted to see Kevin lose his driving licence for longer. Eunice didn't seem to care much and had been keen to tell on Kevin to get her own back for something he'd done. Chris didn't ask what, that was her business. It was obvious she disliked the bloke and any knife she could help push into him would be welcome. Chris wrote down details of where she lived and the registration number of her Cortina. She asked him to let her know what happened. He said he would.

Chris looked out of the window at the bus stop and saw Liz walking towards it. He'd almost forgotten about her. When was the last time he'd seen her? Not since they'd been to bed, just over a week ago. Her blonde hair seemed to stand out in the grey morning and he realised he still fancied her. It was a pity you couldn't go out with two women at the same time without having to lie.

Chris heard the toilet door open and Bill walk down the corridor towards him.

'Follow me young man,' Bill said. Chris followed him downstairs to his room.

Bill got out his little video camcorder and showed Chris how to use it.

'I presume Rachel has a video of her own? You don't want to use my room as well to play it back?'

'No, she's got one of her own.'

'Well, you need this adaptor too. You plug it into the video like this.' Bill knelt down at the side of his machine. 'Press this button here and off you go. The tape's thirty minutes long. Will that be enough?'

'Let me have a spare one as well, will you?'

'Okay. And for fucks sake don't drop the thing. If you do it'll be the most expensive rental you've ever had.'

'I won't.'

'And don't get pissed before you do it either. It's almost impossible when you start to keep the thing steady. Any slight movement and the picture jumps about. It looks awful and takes a lot of practice. Those TV men must have arms of steel.'

'Thanks Bill. I'll buy you a bottle of something.'

Chris went back to his room and put the camera on his bed.

The next thing he did was call Kevin. He had to use the telephone in the foyer which wasn't ideal because people were always walking through. Plus it was right next to reception. He'd been given Kevin's number by Leo. He dialled it and felt the nerves in his stomach as he listened to it ring.

'Yeah?' was the first thing Kevin said when he picked it up.

'Is that Kevin Jenkins?' Chris asked.

'Yeah.'

'You don't know me,' Chris said, 'but I've got a video of you driving a stolen light blue Cortina last Saturday. Registration number HGE 435M. I happen to know that you're not legally entitled to drive a car and I wondered if you'd be willing to buy the video off me.'

The line went silent and then Kevin said: 'What the fuck're you on about? Who are you?'

'You heard what I said. Now what I'm looking for is about two thousand pounds. I think that should be worthwhile. If you don't I'm going to give the video to the police and see if they can use it.' The line was silent again for a few seconds. Chris thought he could hear Kevin breathing, but maybe it was his own breath. There were some apprentices sitting in the hallway but none of them seemed to be listening to him.

'I don't believe you. How did you get a video of me?' Kevin said.

That was almost an admission, Chris thought. He turned his back on the foyer and talked quietly into the phone, looking at the booth wall in front of him where people had scribbled numbers. 'I live in Welling, in Darenth Road. I won't tell you which flat. Last Saturday I got a call from a neighbour telling me she'd had her car stolen. She knew you'd taken it. I agreed to wait in her flat with her until you brought the car back. I videoed you from her window. Then I videoed you walking up the front path. Just before you dropped the envelope through the letter box. We've still got that, with your handwriting on it. Then I videoed you walking away.' Chris paused to let that lot sink in. 'This could be quite costly to you. Not only stealing a car but driving without a licence.'

'Well aren't you the clever dick. Where the fuck am I going to get two grand from?' Kevin's voice was getting desperate.

'You'll find it,' Chris said. He didn't want to mention the robbery because that would implicate Leo.

'And how do I get this money to you?'

'You meet me at the Boroughheath Shopping Mall at five o'clock. On the roof. Take the lift to the second floor where the Gents is. Next to the Gents there's a door that says Management Offices. You walk through that and down a corridor. No one will stop you. At the end of the corridor you come out on the roof. I'll be waiting there for you. I'll be wearing a balaclava.'

'Very clever.'

'Well, I don't want you to see my face do I? You may have thoughts of revenge.' Chris could almost hear Kevin cracking up. He knew he had the bastard.

'I'll be there,' Kevin said eventually, and hung up.

Chris put the phone down and breathed out. He'd never pulled anything like that before and he was feeling pretty good, although his hand was shaking. He picked up the phone again and dialled Leo's number.

*

When Kevin put the phone down he started swearing. He could feel a temper welling up inside him and he stood there mouthing off every swear word he could think of. He looked around the room for something to throw, and then walked over to the door and started hitting it. He pounded it with the base of his fist to get rid of his frustration. When he'd tired of that, he went to his father's drinks cabinet and took out a bottle of Teachers. He unscrewed the top and took a long swig. Then he put the cap back on and threw the bottle at one of the walls. It smashed in an explosion of glass and brown liquid. He walked to the wall and started licking it, some shards of glass going on to his tongue as well. He didn't care if they cut his insides to shreds. On the floor lay the base of the bottle with the Teachers label hanging off it. Kevin didn't like whisky much. If it had been Remy Martin he probably wouldn't have thrown it. He knelt down and picked up the bottle and started stroking his wrist with the rough broken edge. It would be so easy to dig it in there. Then with the thought of that he started to calm down. Things might be desperate but he wasn't ready to die yet. He lay the bottle back on the floor and stood up. Then he went upstairs to get dressed.

*

Chris was sitting with Leo in the saloon bar of The Sydney Arms, the pub in Elmhurst where he'd met Liz the night he'd slept with her. Leo had caught a bus out and Chris had met him at the bus stop. Leo had never been to Elmhurst before, only through it. Chris found that pretty amazing. It was only about four miles from where Leo lived.

'It's because of its reputation,' Leo said. 'This is a rich area. What would I want to drink in a pub full of yuppies for?'

'How many yuppies can you see in here?' Chris asked.

Leo looked around. 'Quite a few actually.'

'You're right,' Chris had to admit. 'You have to learn to ignore them, though.'

Then they started talking about their plans for the meeting with Kevin. Chris was drinking orange juice and he'd told Leo to order something soft too. He wanted them both to be alert, not suffering from post afternoon drinking drowsiness. Chris told Leo how he'd come up with the video idea.

'I got it from a story in a newspaper,' Chris said. 'This was a couple of weeks ago. There was this father whose son was killed by a drunk driver back in '86. The driver was put in jail for nine months and banned from driving for four and a half years. He came out of jail, and before his ban was finished, he started driving again. He was caught and banned for a further three years, but he still carried on driving.'

'Sounds like an idiot.'

'Well, he had his own company you see, so he needed transport to run it. Anyway, the father finds out from someone that this bloke's back on the road. They live in the same town. The father's retired – in his late sixties. He thinks right, I'm going to nobble this bastard. He owns a van and he converts it into a mobile film unit. I presume he drills peep holes in the side or something. He puts a camp bed in there too and some food supplies. Then he parks outside the bloke's house for hours on end and takes video film and a few photographs of him driving to work.'

'Smart.'

'He does this for months, gets a nice load of footage, and then hands it in to the police. The bloke's hauled in again and charged with drinking and driving for the third time.'

'They must've banned him for life.'

'Well no, they didn't actually. The judge – and you've got to admit there are some pretty senile judges in this country – the judge bans him for just one more year, saying he appreciated the difficulties the bloke would have running his pebble-dash business without a car.'

'But that's the whole point!'

'So the father walks from court fuming. Imagine how he feels. He's probably back in his van taking more film right now.'

'Poor bastard.'

'But that's what gave me the idea. I pretended to Kevin that I videoed him driving the stolen Cortina, and threatened to give it to the police. I'll give him a blank video in exchange for two grand.'

Leo was smiling. 'You think he'll fall for that?'

'He's got no choice. He can't risk it.'

'Why only two grand? He's got two and a half.'

'That would look a little obvious wouldn't it, if I asked him for the exact amount he's got?'

Leo nodded. 'I suppose so.'

'Plus, if we leave him with five hundred to play with he's less likely to try something. He should be satisfied just to cut his losses. At least he's not ending up empty handed.'

'And where do I come into all this?'

'You're going to take the video camera on to the roof with us and film my meeting with Kevin. That way, if he does try something we'll definitely have him. He might try and attack me for instance. If he does I want it on film.'

'You don't miss much do you? Are those things easy to work? I've never shot any film before.'

'You just press a button and hold it. Just keep a steady hand. We'll get there early and find you a decent hiding place.'

'What if someone comes along?'

'It's pretty quiet up there. The roof's used for shop deliveries. You get lorries going up there and unloading, but there's never many people walking around.'

'I hope not.'

'Don't worry about it. I'll be doing the hard bit.'

Leo sipped his orange juice. 'And how do we split the money up this time?'

Chris grinned. 'Don't you trust me?'

'Not a bit.'

'Well, you get another five hundred to add to the two fifty you've already got. Five hundred's not bad for the hours work you're going to do. Then I'll give Eunice a couple of hundred for getting us the information and keep the rest for myself.'

Dashy thought about that for a moment. 'That's thirteen hundred for you. That's a bit steep.'

'I'm the one who thought up the plan. I'm also the one with the injuries.'

'I suppose so. Do you have to give anything to Eunice?'

'Just a bit to keep her quiet.'

'Two hundred seems a lot.'

'I'm a generous guy.'

'Yeah. I knew that the first time I met you.'

'And when it's all finished we'll never see each other again.'

'Fair enough.'

Chris finished his drink and nodded at Leo's empty glass. 'You want another of those?'

Leo turned his nose up. 'I wouldn't mind something stronger.'

'It's orange juice or nothing.'

Leo reluctantly handed his glass over and Chris went to the bar.

Nineteen

Dashy got into the Shopping Mall lift with Chris. He had the video camera in a leather overnight bag of Chris's, while Chris had the spare blank video tape in his jacket pocket. They stood apart in the lift as if they didn't know each other. Dashy didn't feel like talking anyway. He was getting as nervous as the night he'd mugged Chris. He looked at the other people in the lift who had been talking a minute earlier outside but were now completely silent. He looked up at the floor numbers above the door.

When the lift stopped on the second floor Dashy followed Chris out. They walked across the landing to the Management Office door. Dashy heard the lift closing behind them as they pushed through the doors.

They came to a carpeted corridor and Chris still didn't speak. Dashy had never been through here before and he wondered how Chris knew about it. The bloke was full of surprises.

As they walked along, Dashy looked at the pictures on the walls. They were framed aerial photographs of the Mall at various stages of construction. The further they went along the corridor the more the building in the pictures started taking shape. At the entrance, the aerial photograph was of a patch of rubble-laden land. Then foundations appeared, then scaffolding and walls, and as they rounded a corner to the receptionist's there was a larger photograph of the completed Mall. Dashy was so engrossed in the pictures that he didn't notice a girl looking at him from behind a desk loaded down with potted plants. Chris, as cool as you like, just smiled at her, said hello, and walked past. Dashy nodded at the girl but she had already gone back to her newspaper.

The next part of the corridor wasn't as well lit and on the ceiling ahead was a sign pointing to a doorway marked Security. Dashy was getting even more nervous. There was a camera up there, too. Were they being recorded on video? He had seen those clips on *Crimewatch* where robbers had been photographed in building societies. He could just imagine himself sitting at home, watching the programme with his parents, when his face comes up on the screen. Do you know this man? Do you know where he's living? If so, call this number. Dashy ran up to Chris and patted him on the shoulder.

'There's a fucking camera up there!' he said.

'Don't worry about it. It's only some nut falling asleep in front of about twenty screens.'

'Don't they keep the film though?'

'I don't think so. They keep the film they take of the Mall inside. For shoplifters and the like. But I wouldn't have thought they'd keep it for these corridors.'

But Dashy noticed the look of doubt on Chris's face. What else wasn't he sure of? Was this going to turn into one almighty cock-up? As they walked past the Security door, Dashy looked through it. There was a narrow corridor and another camera. It didn't look too welcoming. Probably led to an interrogation room with bright lights. He hurried along.

The corridor ended and they came out on the roof. It was almost dark outside, but the perimeter of the roof was lit. Just light enough for Dashy to take some video film.

'This is where Kevin'll come out,' Chris said, 'so I'm going to be waiting here for him. Now let's find a good place for you.'

Dashy looked at the roof. It was a large tarmacked area with cars parked along the right hand side and loading bays for shops on the other sides. These were kept clear so the lorries could get in and out easily. In the far right corner was a ramp going down to the entrance. It was windy up there and Dashy wasn't sure whether it was that that made him shiver, or the situation he was in. He looked at Chris.

'It seems pretty quiet,' he said.

'It always is this time of day. No one delivers this late. The only people around are the cleaners. They keep the rubbish bins around to the right there.' Chris pointed and Dashy noticed the roof continued round the corner of the building. This was obviously just half the roof.

'I think the best place for you is behind those cars over there,' Chris said.

Dashy looked at the parked cars. 'What if someone leaves to drive home?'

'Just move behind another one. You've got good visibility from there, so it doesn't matter where you are. If you want to, you could even get under one of them.'

'Sod that. I'm not getting run over for five hundred quid.'

Chris was smiling at him. 'Only joking. We won't be here for long anyway. Twenty minutes with any luck.'

'I'll get over there, then.'

'Good luck,' Chris said.

'And you.'

*

Kevin caught the bus to the Shopping Mall and arrived at four-thirty. For the twenty minutes he had to kill he walked around the Mall looking in shop windows. It reminded him of that day he'd been spying in shops, trying to find the one to rob. When he came to the window of She Girl he had a quick look to see if either of the girls he'd mugged were working. He couldn't, and walked on quickly in case one of them came out and recognised him. Now all that hard work was about to come to nothing. He felt the bulge in his jacket pocket – two thousand in a paper bag. Well at least Dashy wasn't getting any more of it.

After taking a shower and cleaning up the smashed whisky bottle, Kevin had moped around the house, wondering whether he should hand over the rest of the money to his mystery caller or not. He tried to figure out who the caller was, but if he was a friend of Eunice's and lived in her block of flats then he wouldn't know him anyway, and there was little point thinking about it. In the end, he reluctantly decided to hand the money over and end it once and for all. It wasn't worth the risk of losing his driving licence for longer; and he still had five hundred for himself. He could go back to the betting shop – a different one, so he wouldn't bump into Dashy – place a few bets, and hopefully make the five hundred grow a little.

Kevin planned another little surprise, as well. Instead of following the directions he'd been given, he intended to go up to the Mall roof by a different route, hoping to catch the blackmailer unawares and see who it was. Instead of going up in the lift to the Management Offices, he pushed through a Staff Only door next to one of the shops. He found himself in a long concrete corridor.

He walked quickly along the corridor feeling a little spooky. Above him there was a tangle of grey pipes, probably something to do with the Mall heating. There were cream-painted doors in the corridor, obviously leading into the backs of shops, although no shop names were painted on them. At the end of the corridor he had to turn left and walk another thirty yards or so. The corridor turned twice more and Kevin wondered if he was just going round in a circle. Eventually it ended, and he pushed through some fire doors to find himself at the bottom of a flight of stone stairs. He started climbing them.

At the top of the stairs – a long haul – were more fire doors, and pushing through them Kevin ended up in... another corridor! He walked quickly, fearing he'd get lost and miss his meeting. He passed more shop back-doors, but this time they were dark brown. Small cameras hung periodically from the ceiling and that really worried him. He imagined a bunch of those thick security guards huddled around a TV screen laughing at his antics. He started to regret coming this way after all. He started to sweat. If he ever got to the roof, he'd arrive there with no composure left.

After turning another bend in the corridor, Kevin eventually saw the roof. He breathed a sigh of relief and slowed down. He looked at his watch. It was five-past-five. He walked slowly up to the opening and looked out.

*

Chris was getting nervous on the roof, sitting on a foot high concrete step that stopped delivery trucks from backing into the wall. It was five o'clock and from where he sat he could see right down the corridor Kevin should be coming through. Outside it was getting darker by the minute.

Chris was wearing a dark blue woollen hat he'd owned for years. He seldom wore it because it was too big for him: when fully unrolled, it covered the whole of his face. After his telephone conversation with Kevin, Chris had gone back to his room and cut two holes in it. When he saw Kevin coming down the corridor, he aimed to pull it down over his eyes. He would have preferred to be wearing it like that from the start, but it would have looked a little suspicious to anyone walking by. The sort of thing someone would remember later, if questioned. He'd already had one of the cleaners walk by and notice him sitting there.

Chris had been on the roof only once before, about a year ago. Being naturally nosy, he'd begun one lunchtime when he'd had nothing to do, walking down the corridor he and Leo had just come along. No one had stopped him, so he'd walked right out on to the roof and explored the whole area. He had been amazed at how quiet it was. When he'd needed a venue for the showdown with Kevin, the roof was the first place that sprang to mind. But he had forgotten about the security cameras along the corridor.

Chris looked at his watch. He didn't expect Kevin to necessarily be on time, but he expected him to turn up. He looked across the roof to see if Leo was there. He scanned the parked cars and saw Leo's feet moving underneath and behind one of them. He couldn't see the camera though. He hoped Leo wouldn't fuck it up. There was always the chance something would go wrong, and they needed the film for a little extra leverage. But if everything went to plan, he could wipe the tape and give it straight back to Bill. He'd only have to remember to buy Bill a new tape to replace the blank he was about to give Kevin.

It was cold waiting on the roof and a lot windier than on the street. Chris huddled into his coat and thought of the money that would soon be his, hoping those kind of thoughts would keep him warm. They just made him colder though. For a second, he wondered if he should wave Leo over and call the whole thing off. What the hell was he messing with here, anyway? He was about to step from a relatively normal life into the world of smalltime crime, with the risk of getting into serious trouble and a criminal record. Maybe even jail. Why was he doing it? Okay, so he'd done some thieving before, stealing a few LPs here and there, but money was always different. And what happened when he got the money? Would he want to go out and pull something again, or would it be enough to satisfy him? He didn't know, and quite frankly, he didn't want to think about it too much. All he knew for sure was that he wasn't getting anywhere with his life, making menial money in the off-licence, and the thirteen hundred pounds would be a way of cutting a few corners. Plus the two-fifty he already had of course. Speed up the process of living. Better to worry about it afterwards.

Chris looked at his feet, thinking maybe he'd buy himself a new pair of trainers. Then he heard a shuffle behind him, and before he could turn, felt an arm around his neck! The arm tightened and pulled him backwards off the concrete ledge, and before he knew it, Kevin was on top of him and had his hands around his throat.

'So it was you, you bastard!' Kevin was saying.

He was gripping so tightly Chris couldn't reply. Mostly he was trying to concentrate on breathing. Kevin suddenly started whacking his head down hard on to the tarmac and Chris couldn't make out his words at all, just saw his lips moving like something out of a bad dream. Then, as quickly as it had started, Kevin had let go and was on his feet. Chris looked up and saw Leo running towards them shouting, the video camera in one hand.

Kevin took one look at Leo and started running across the tarmac, around the corner and to the other side of the roof. Chris watched Leo follow and groggily got to his feet. He started jogging after them.

The other side of the roof was where the Mall's cleaners were based. They kept their wheeled orange and grey rubbish bins – each about five feet long by four deep – in a large alcove, ready to be trundled to the back of the shops each day to be filled. Chris ran the fifty yards to the alcove feeling things that he'd felt the night he'd been mugged; it was like being in a game of rugby again, only this time he was running down the wing to score. And this time his legs felt like lead. He couldn't see Leo and Kevin as he ran, and wondered if they'd turned left and veered down the exit ramp. But when Chris reached the alcove, struggling for breath, he saw Kevin lying on the ground by the side of a row of parked bins. Leo was kneeling beside him, the video camera on the tarmac by his leg.

'What happened?' Chris said, forcing the words out of his throat.

Dashy looked up at him and there were tears running down his cheeks. 'He's dead. The idiot's dead!'

Chris walked over and knelt beside Leo. Kevin's head was at an awkward angle, against one of the bins. Chris grabbed a wrist and felt for a pulse; he didn't really know where to feel, so he just grabbed the entire wrist. Then he flung his hand around Kevin's neck and felt there. There was no movement. He unzipped Kevin's jacket, pulled his pullover out of the way, and inspected his bare stomach for breathing movement. Nothing. He pushed the pullover back down and looked at Leo.

Leo was sobbing now, the tears rolling freely down his cheeks, his face creased in pain. Chris looked inside Kevin's jacket for the money. He found it in a paper bag, stuffed it in his jacket pocket and stood up. He pulled opened the lid on one of the rubbish bins and asked Leo to give him a hand.

Leo slowly got to his feet and together they lifted Kevin's body up and dumped it in the bin. Chris took some cardboard from a pile nearby and covered Kevin with it, before shutting the lid. He bent down and picked up the video camera. Leo was shaking, looking down at the ground, the tears still falling.

'Let's get out of here,' Chris said. 'Dry your face. Here.' He handed Leo a handkerchief.

'Where's my leather bag?' he asked Leo.

'Back at the cars.'

'You see that door over there?' Chris pointed. 'Go through it and keep walking. Those corridors all lead out to the street. If you see anyone, just smile at them and say good evening. I'll meet you outside the bookies in ten minutes. I'm going back for the bag.'

'Okay.'

'Now go.' Chris pushed Leo in the right direction and walked back to the parked cars for his bag. He heard a soft whirring sound and thought it was coming from his head. Then he realised it was coming from his hand. He looked at the video camera and noticed it was still running. He reached down and shut it off.

Twenty

On the bus ride back to the YMCA, Chris couldn't stop his hands from shaking. Just like the night he'd been mugged. Nerves were running through his stomach, making him want to vomit. He was sitting on the top deck in the back seat, the bus full of shouting schoolkids and people going home from work. He had already rewound the video tape and now it was recording the blackness of the inside of his bag. He wanted to wipe everything that took place on the Mall roof for good.

He'd got away safely from The Mall and had met Leo outside the bookies, as arranged. Leo had been standing there, the tears dried up, but his head bowed, looking at the pavement, a mask of extreme sadness on his face. Chris didn't think he'd ever seen such a look before. He walked up to Leo, patted him on the arm, and together they walked slowly down the High Street. For a long time Leo didn't say anything, and Chris was trying to work out what to do next. They walked into the darkness of Danson Park and sat on a bench. Chris stayed silent for a while and asked Leo what had happened. He had to ask again before Leo told him.

'I was running after him,' Leo said, looking at his hands, twisting them around each other, 'and I swung the camera and caught him on the back of the head. It wasn't a hard blow, but the next thing I know, he's falling forward and crashed into those bins. I think he broke his neck when he hit the bins.'

'Shit,' Chris said.

'So that's that,' Leo said.

'That's what?'

'The complete fuck-up that's my life.'

Chris looked at Leo and felt guilty. If it hadn't been for him, Leo wouldn't have been in such a mess. He should've just reported him for the mugging and not got involved. Now Leo would probably get done for manslaughter and Chris would get some sort of suspended sentence as his accomplice. Both their lives would be ruined. Chris didn't care about himself so much because he always felt confident enough to get by, no matter what, but what about Leo? Even if he survived his term in jail – which Chris doubted – he'd never be able to find work again. He'd end up on the streets, one of the many homeless people hanging around the West End.

Chris said then: 'Can anyone tie you to Kevin? Is there anyone who knows you know him?'

'Only his father. He met me once. I talked with him for five minutes.'

'Would he remember your name?'

'I don't know. Maybe.'

'Okay. This is what we do. You go home and act as normal. Tell your mother you've been at the bookies all day. And just lie low. Go to the Job Centre tomorrow, go to the bookies, do what you normally do. The body'll be discovered tomorrow, then they'll go to his father, and if he remembers you, they'll come and see you. You may be safe for a day or two.'

'Great.'

'I'll hang on to the money. We don't want it tied to you in any way.'

'I don't want it.'

'If the cops do come and ask about Kevin, tell them the truth. You knew him, you went betting with him. But you hadn't seen him for a few days. If you deny everything I don't see what they can pin on you.' Chris wished he felt as confident as he sounded.

'That's if they haven't got us on film,' Leo said.

'What do you mean?'

'Those corridors. Those cameras gave me the shits as soon as I saw them. I knew we should've left right then.'

Chris wished they had, too, even though he was pretty sure the cameras didn't record anything. Hopefully there wasn't a security guard glued to the screen when they'd walked through. It all came down to luck. If they got the breaks, they could get away with it.

'I'm going home now,' Chris said then. 'Only call me if you're in trouble. Call me at the shop.'

Leo nodded. Chris stood up. He felt like shaking hands with Leo but it seemed inappropriate. He doubted if he'd ever see him again – that's if he didn't see him in court.

'Go home Leo,' he said. 'It was just bad luck. It wasn't your fault.' He patted him on the shoulder and walked away.

Now, Chris was looking at the passing houses from the upper-deck bus window. It was a route he'd taken many times, twice a day for two years, but he somehow felt that he was seeing things for the first time. He looked in to the lit front windows as they passed, at the comfortable chairs and the glowing TV sets. He realised that such a homely setting would be out of his grasp for a good many years yet, maybe even forever. Was that a situation he'd ever reach, or was it something he even wanted? He didn't know. All he did know was that right now he'd rather be in one of those houses than riding back to the YMCA on the bus, with a whole pile of trouble awaiting him in the next few days.

When his stop eventually arrived, Chris struggled to his feet and walked shakily down the stairs. He climbed off and headed for the YMCA.

Back in the safety of his room, he took the video camera out of the bag and had a look at it. He was looking for traces of blood from Kevin's head but couldn't see any. Thankfully, nothing had been broken by the impact. Surely Leo couldn't have hit him that hard. It must've been the speed Kevin was running at that had made him hit the bins so fatally. If you were running fast, it didn't take much to knock you over. Chris rewound the tape he had just erased and put the camera on his desk. He'd give it to Bill later. Right now he needed a shower. He stripped off and walked down the corridor in his dressing gown.

One of the things Chris would miss about the YMCA – the only thing he would miss, Christ! he was beginning to think like a condemned man already – was the showers. He had never lived anywhere that had a shower before, and he loved standing underneath them, letting hot water blast over his shoulders.

All the bathrooms consisted of two shower cubicles and a bath – which Chris had never used – all with lockable doors. Chris locked himself in to a shower room and turned on the water. He scrubbed himself hard to get rid of the sweat from his body. Where had all that come from? Fear? The back of his head was sore from where Kevin had banged it on the tarmac roof. His throat felt sore as well from Kevin's attempted strangulation. He was almost getting used to being bashed around and it really didn't bother him one way or the other now. In fact it made him feel tough, gave him a slight thrill, although he doubted he'd be feeling that way if Kevin had stuck him with a knife.

After ten minutes, Chris turned off the shower and stepped on to the brown tile floor. Someone knocked on the locked door.

'Yeah?'

'Chris?'

'Yeah?'

'It's Liz.'

Chris wrapped a towel around his middle, unlocked the door, and there was Liz in her jeans and crimson leather jacket, her short blonde hair tied up in a ribbon.

'Well, hello.'

'I tried your door but didn't get an answer. They said you were in at reception. So I thought you must be around.'

'How are you?'

'Fine.' Now she was looking at Chris's body.

'Do you want to join me?' he asked.

Liz laughed. 'You're all wet.'

'That's the idea.' Chris could see her thinking about it. He was feeling in a reckless mood. He was in enough trouble already, he couldn't get in much more.

'We might get caught.'

'That's the idea,' Chris said again. But he saw Liz hesitate so he picked up his things and motioned her back to his room. She followed him down the corridor as he padded along in his wet flip-flops.

'Come and watch me get dressed,' he winked, and Liz followed him in.

With the door shut behind them, Chris let his towel fall and started drying himself in front of her. Liz sat down in the armchair and watched.

'You're not a shy person are you?' she said.

'You never get anywhere by being shy. Be forthright, that's my motto. Anyway, what brings you here?'

'Nothing, really. I just popped in to see you. I've not seen you for ages.'

'Not since we were in this room together.'

'Eight days ago.'

'It seems like longer.'

Liz was looking at him. Chris was starting to get hard. It wasn't an easy thing to cover up.

'Don't you feel over-dressed?' he asked.

'Very.'

Liz stood up and started taking off her clothes. In a few minutes she was naked too. They looked at each other and hesitated.

'What now?' Chris asked.

*

They lay under the sheets together in the narrow single bed. Chris was thinking how easy it was. First Liz last Tuesday, then Rachel on Sunday, and now Liz again on Wednesday. It was a lifestyle he could get used to. That's if he had any lifestyle left.

'Are we going to carry on like this,' Liz asked. 'Or shall we make a go of it?'

'You mean boy and girlfriend?'

'Yes.'

'Give me a couple of days.'

'That's what you said last time.'

'Was it?'

'You said give me a couple of days to think things over and I'll give you a ring. The telephone kind, that is.'

'I don't remember that.'

'You weren't exactly sober.'

'Neither were you.'

'No, I wasn't.'

Liz stopped talking. The less talk Chris heard about future plans the better. Right now he couldn't plan beyond this evening. He looked at the bedside clock. It was nearly seven.

'I've missed my evening meal, thanks to you,' he said. 'Do you feel like eating out?'

'Yes. Let's get up.'

They got dressed and Chris tried to make himself look presentable. But no matter what he did after sex, he always looked different. Rough and untidy. His hair was a tangled mess and he couldn't get it to look neat. His head still had a dull ache from Kevin's bashing. What made it worse was that Liz looked impeccable. Maybe he should've been going out with her in the first place.

They left Chris's room and walked along to the foyer. Liz got admiring looks from the young apprentices sitting there. She was the type it felt good to walk beside whereas Rachel was the type it felt good to be with. Maybe he should be concentrating on Rachel.

They walked up the driveway holding hands, trees and a school playing field on their left, the half-sized football pitch on their right. Liz told him it was a creepy road.

'Anything could happen to you down here,' she said.

'Not to me. Blokes are safe.'

That was the wrong thing to say right then because Chris saw Rachel walk off the main road and head down the drive towards them. He let go of Liz's hand.

'Here comes trouble,' he said. Liz looked at him. 'This is the reason I can't go out with you. My girlfriend Rachel.'

Liz looked at Rachel approaching and said, 'This should be fun.'

When Rachel reached them, she had a funny look on her face. She stared at Liz. Chris said hello and asked her what she was doing there.

'A policeman came in to the shop see you,' she said. 'I thought I'd come and tell you.' She looked at Liz again. 'I wish I hadn't now.'

'Did he say what he wanted?'

'No. He was in uniform. Not that one we saw the other day.'

Chris was relieved. Maybe it was about something else. Maybe something to do with shoplifters. But they wouldn't have asked for him, would they? Ron could've sorted it out.

'Are you on your way out?' Rachel asked him.

Chris introduced Liz to her. 'She's a friend of Bill's,' he added. Then he realised Rachel didn't know who Bill was. 'He's a friend of mine that lives here. We're just going up the pub to try and find him.'

'Actually,' Liz said, 'I'm Chris's other piece of stuff. We've just been to bed together and we were going for a meal. But now that we've met, I think I'll go home instead.' She smiled at Chris, a quick one that she snapped off straight away, and then walked off.

Chris looked at Rachel. She had started to cry. She was the second person he'd brought to tears in the last couple of hours.

'Now you know,' he said. 'If it makes it any easier, we've known each other about two weeks. I've only seen her twice.'

'You mean slept with her. That's once more than me.'

Chris tried to put his arms around her but she pushed him

away. 'I hope you'll find it easy coming into work tomorrow,' she said. 'Because I'll still be there.'

Then she walked away from him as well. Chris watched her for a minute and then turned back to the YMCA. Well, what else could happen to him today?

*

After Chris had left him in Danson Park, Dashy had stayed on the cold bench and chain-smoked for thirty minutes. He waited until he felt cold, until he was shivering and feeling uncomfortable. If he could make himself numb with cold, maybe he could numb his mind as well; his mind was starting to think awful things, things he had thought about before but had always managed to shut out. He got a few looks from passers-by, people on their way home from work, but he really didn't give a fuck about them. He'd been through too much for them to understand, and in a way, he felt superior. But he also felt inferior.

Sitting there in the park, he thought of Kevin's body, and pictured it lying against the orange and grey rubbish bin. He went through the events leading up to his death, the sprint along the roof, the swinging of the video camera, the easy way Kevin had fallen, easier than Dashy would ever have imagined.

Kevin was the second dead person he had seen in 1992. And there was still December to come.

In a trance-like state, he got up from the bench and started walking home. Twenty minutes later, he'd reached his street and was looking at the semi-detached houses, wondering how people coped with day to day living; was everyone happy or were they all miserable like him? What was the point of it all? He opened the front door quietly and went straight to his room. He could hear his mother in the kitchen as he climbed the stairs. The sound of the TV drifted up from the living room, and he knew his father would be in there watching the news. His father was a news addict for reasons that escaped Dashy. Current affairs bored him silly. He had enough problems of his own not to be worried about world affairs.

Once inside his bedroom, with the lights on and the door locked, Dashy tried to relax. He sat on the bed and looked at the pictures on the walls – the sports stars. All he had ever wanted in life was to be good at one sport. If he had been good at football he wouldn't have asked for anything more, but at school he had been too clumsy to be good at any sport. Okay, so he was big and strong, but football needed a bit of finesse. Sometimes he wished he'd gone to a rugby-playing school, then maybe his bulk could've been put to use in the scrum. It was too late, though. At twenty-five you were halfway through your sporting life. If Danny were still alive, he would still have a chance. But Danny hadn't been much good at sport either. He had been too small and skinny, the brunt of much taunting at school. Dashy had always suspected that school was the real reason Danny had killed himself. He was getting bullied, and then coming back in the evenings to a home where no one talked or took an interest in anything. Except for Dashy, of course. He had always talked to Danny. But why had Danny never opened up to him about his problems? Was he unapproachable? Did Danny feel ashamed because Dashy would never be the type to be bullied? Dashy reasoned that might be true. He felt even more depressed. He lay down on his bed and buried his head in his pillow and started to cry.

A few minutes later his mother knocked on the door.

'Are you in there, Leo?' she called.

Dashy took his head out of the pillow and answered, yes.

'It's time for supper. Wash your hands and come down.'

'Okay,' Dashy said. He started to dry his eyes on the pillow. Leo. His mother always called him Leo. His dad never called him anything except son, and Chris was the only other person who called him Leo. Everyone else called him Dashy. Fucking Dashy. Sometimes Leo didn't know who the hell he was any more.

Twenty One

Chris woke up the next morning on his bed, fully clothed. It was the maid who stirred him, coming in at eight o'clock to tidy the room. After losing both Liz and Rachel, he had spent the previous evening in his room with the lights out. He had drunk half a bottle of whisky and was feeling the effects.

'Sorry,' the maid said.

Chris looked up at her through half-closed eyes and a pounding head. 'It's okay. I was just leaving.'

'I'll come back in a minute.' The maid left.

Chris struggled to his feet and drank a glass of water. Then he left his room, walked upstairs to the TV room, and switched on the set. He sat in a chair in the back row and watched Breakfast TV. He put his head on the back of the seat and fell asleep again.

He woke up half an hour later confronted by the weatherman. Chris envied him. He had such a reassuring voice, kindly face and manner, and he seemed to derive such pleasure from telling people about wind and rain. Chris wished he could find a job that paid well and that would keep him interested for twenty years. Did such a job exist? He'd already decided he wasn't going in to the off-licence today, and probably wouldn't go back at all. Apart from having to face Rachel, he was sick of Ron and his chicken tikka sandwiches, and sick of working in a shop, period. It would soon be Christmas, and the thought of all those busy days ahead, trying to please obnoxious customers appalled him. How had he managed it for two years?

He stood up and switched off the TV. His room would be ready now, and he knew he should be thinking about the day ahead.

But he couldn't.

He sat for an hour in his room and didn't know what to do. His headache had subsided, thanks to three aspirin, but he was feeling restless and nervous. Ideally, he would just like to pack a suitcase and go away somewhere for a while. But wouldn't that look suspicious if Morgan came round to see him? Chris didn't know. For the first time since he'd split up with Amanda he wished she were there, so that he could ask her advice. If he were still living with her, none of this would've happened. Okay, so he still would've been mugged, but she would've told him to forget it. He could be sitting now in a nice comfortable flat with Amanda's homely decorations, instead of this bare, cold-looking YMCA room. But then again, all those things were what he'd been tiring of. He'd been getting too soft. But look where being tough got you.

He stood up and pulled down a suitcase from on top of the wardrobe. He lay it on the bed and started packing enough clothes for a week's holiday. Finally, he put in a towel and his washing things. He would pay a week's rent before he left, catch a bus to the station, and a train up to London. Then he would go to Victoria coach station, pick a destination and just go. He didn't mind where he ended up, as long as it was far away and preferably up north. He'd find a bed and breakfast and lie low for a while.

He opened his desk drawer and took out the paper bag with Kevin's money in it. Along with the two hundred and fifty from Leo's first payment, he'd got quite a nice little bundle. He counted out three hundred pounds, enough to have a good holiday with, and another sixty to pay his rent. Then he found two large brown envelopes. He addressed one to Eunice and put two hundred pounds inside. He addressed the other to Amanda and put over a thousand pounds inside that one. Then he carried them both to reception.

Sitting behind the window was another YMCA employee Chris had hardly spoken to before. He was a young lad with a stupid-looking face, round glasses, and terrible smelling feet. Even facing him through the cubby hole Chris could smell his socks. That was one very good reason why Chris had never lingered to talk with him.

'Can you post these for me?' Chris asked, handing him the bulky envelopes. 'Recorded delivery. Here's a tenner for your trouble.'

'Sure thing!' said the boy.

'I want to pay my rent as well,' Chris said.

'Sure thing.'

Chris handed over his sixty pounds and watched as the boy entered it in the book and gave him a receipt.

'What time will those go?' Chris asked, pointing to his letters.

The boy looked at his watch. 'I'll go to the post office in about half an hour. I've got some others to take as well.'

'Don't forget. Recorded delivery. They're very important.'

'I won't.'

Chris watched the boy pick up a small brown sack and drop the letters in.

'Okay?' the boy said.

'Sure thing,' Chris said, and walked back to his room.

Now if he was caught, which he was beginning to think was the most likely outcome, at least his money would be safe with Amanda. She would recognise his writing on the envelope. She wouldn't know where he'd got it from, but if she thought back to the time she'd seen him leaving the pub with Leo, she'd be able to work it out. And Chris knew she wouldn't hand the money in. Amanda would either hang on to it for him, or put the money to use. Chris hoped she'd put it towards the house she'd always wanted to buy. That way at least some good would come from the whole messy affair. And what if the cops asked Chris where the money was? He'd just say Kevin didn't have it on him when he was killed.

Back in his room, Chris locked his suitcase, picked up his coat, and left. He walked down the corridor, wondering if it would be the last time. How long would it take the cops to find him? He reckoned he could keep them out of his hair for a week, but they'd be waiting for him when he came back. Or maybe they wouldn't. Maybe he'd come back and everything would've blown over. As he walked through the foyer, the young lad looked at him from the cubby hole. He gave Chris a funny look. Chris ignored him.

He pushed through the swing doors and started walking up the driveway. It was a cool, clear day, warmer than usual, a perfect day for travelling. A perfect day for sitting on a coach looking out the window.

He was about halfway up the driveway when he saw a car turning in off the main road. It drove slowly towards him, lurching over the sleeping policemen in the road. Every time the car bumped Chris could feel his spirits dropping lower. Eventually the car was next to him, Detective Sergeant Morgan in the passenger seat winding his window down. Another plainclothes-man was driving.

'Going somewhere?' Morgan asked.

'I was thinking about it,' Chris said.

'Think again. You're in a lot of trouble.'

'Why's that?'

'You know why.'

'Tell me.'

'Get in the car.'

'Can't you tell me first?'

Morgan gave Chris a tired look. Then a toughness came into his face. He didn't look so much like Dennis Weaver now. 'You either get in the car now, or I get out and put you in,' he said.

Chris thought about it a second and said, 'Okay.'

Morgan reached behind and opened the back door for him. Chris put his suitcase in first, and then climbed inside.

'You can turn round a bit further down,' Morgan told his driver. Chris sat in silence as they drove past reception and turned around in the parking area. Chris looked through the glass doors and saw one of the maids plugging a vacuum cleaner in. Then Morgan turned slowly in his seat and looked at him.

'We got a telephone call from a Mr Dash this morning,' he said. 'He got up for work this morning, went into the kitchen, and looked out of his window. He saw the door to his garden shed was open, so he went down to close it. Do you know what he found in there?'

'I haven't a clue,' Chris said. Now they were going back up the driveway.

'Your friend Leo Dash was hanging from one of the beams. He topped himself with a piece of rope.'

'Oh, shit,' Chris said.

'It turns out his younger brother did the same thing about six months ago, so his father thought it was something to do with that. Then they found a note in his room explaining the mugging and everything else. I've just had a call come through about Kevin Jenkin's body. Two dead bodies in one morning is not an ideal way to start my day.'

Chris was feeling bad inside. The thoughts were racing around in his head, crashing into each other. He hadn't known about Leo's younger brother. He remembered how sad Leo had looked standing outside the bookies. He should've known there was some other problem in that mixed up head of his. But what could he have done, anyway? Chris's thoughts turned to his own problems. What was he going to get out of this? A suspended sentence? A couple of years? He didn't know how the law worked in such cases.

'What's going to happen to me?' he asked Morgan.

'It depends where the pieces fall,' Morgan said. He was looking out of the window across the school playing-fields. To Chris his voice sounded about the same distance away. 'It depends on how it all falls.'

The car stopped at the main road and the driver waited for a break in the traffic. Chris turned in his seat and looked back at the YMCA, the high wire fence down the driveway, and then the big brick building that looked a lot like a prison.

The place he would end up in would probably look much the same.

BLOODLINES the cutting-edge crime and mystery imprint...

Perhaps She'll Die!
by John B Spencer

Giles could never say 'no' to a woman... any woman. But when he tangled with Celeste, he made a mistake... A bad mistake.

Celeste was married to Harry, and Harry walked a dark side of the street that Giles – with his comfortable lifestyle and fashionable media job – could only imagine in his worst nightmares. And when Harry got involved in nightmares, people had a habit of getting hurt.

Set against the boom and gloom of eighties Britain, *Perhaps She'll Die!* is classic *noir* with a centre as hard as toughened diamond.

ISBN 1 899344 14 4 — £5.99

Fresh Blood
edited by Mike Ripley & Maxim Jakubowski

"Move over Agatha Christie and tell Sherlock the News!" This landmark anthology features the cream of the British New Wave of crime writers: John Harvey, Mark Timlin, Chaz Brenchley, Russell James, Stella Duffy, Ian Rankin, Nicholas Blincoe, Joe Canzius, Denise Danks, John B Spencer, Graeme Gordon, the two editors, and a previously unpublished extract from the late Derek Raymond. Includes an introduction from each author explaining their views on crime fiction in the '90s and a comprehensive foreword on the genre from Angel-creator, Mike Ripley.

ISBN 1 899344 03 9 — £6.99

Quake City
by John B Spencer

The third novel to feature Charley Case, the hard-boiled investigator of the future. But of a future that follows the 'Big One of Ninety-Seven' – the quake that literally rips California apart and makes LA an Island.

"Classic Chandleresque private eye tale, jazzed up by being set in the future... but some things never change – PI Charley Case still has trouble with women and a trusty bottle of bourbon is always at hand. An entertaining addition to the private eye canon."
— John Williams, *Mail on Sunday*

ISBN 1 899344 02 0 — £5.99

Outstanding Paperback Originals from The Do-Not Press:

Will You Hold Me?
by Christopher Kenworthy
Christopher Kenworthy's intense, mood-laden stories expertly explore
the vulnerable under-belly of human emotion. From the sleazy back-
streets of Paris to huddled London bedrooms, his characters inhabit a
world where hope too often turns to despair and where compassion is
rewarded with malice.
Christopher Kenworthy is a writer at the cutting edge of contemporary
fiction, and this is the first collection of his brilliantly original stories.
"The voice is original, plain, pained. The content borders on the gothic.
The effect is to reveal both magic and menace as being present in the ordinary." — Geoff Ryman, author of *Was*
ISBN 1 899344 11 X — £6.99

The Users
by Brian Case
The welcome return of Brian Case's brilliantly original '60s cult classic.
"A remarkable debut" —Anthony Burgess
"Why Case's spiky first novel from 1968 should have languished for
nearly thirty years without a reprint must be one of the enigmas of
modern publishing. Mercilessly funny and swaggeringly self-con-
scious, it could almost be a template for an early Martin Amis."
— *Sunday Times*
ISBN 1 899344 05 5— £5.99

Life In The World Of Women
a collection of vile, dangerous and loving stories **by Maxim Jakubowski**
Maxim Jakubowski's dangerous and erotic stories of war between the
sexes are collected here for the first time, including three major new
pieces. Taking in aspects of crime noir, erotica, romance and gritty
social drama, *Life In The World Of Women* confirms Maxim Jakubowski
as one of Britain's finest and hardest-hitting writers.
"Whatever else it might be – romantic pornography or pornographic
romance – *Life* is a bold experiment in self-mythologising fiction."
— Nicholas Royle, *Time Out*
"Demonstrates that erotic fiction can be amusing, touching, spooky
and even (at least occasionally) elegant. Erotic fiction seems to be
Jakubowski's true metier. These stories have the hard sexy edge of
Henry Miller and the redeeming grief of Jack Kerouac. A first class col-
lection." — Ed Gorman, *Mystery Scene* (USA)
ISBN 1 899344 06 3 — £6.99

Outstanding Paperback Originals from The Do-Not Press:

A Two Hander
collected poetry by Sara Kestelman & Susan Penhaligon
A new and impressive collection of poetry from two of Britain's most celebrated actresses. Although their careers have sometimes taken different paths, Sara Kestelman and Susan Penhaligon have come together to write poetry touching on every aspect of their separate lives as women, lovers and actresses. The result is a refreshing mix of styles and subjects, with each writer complementing the other perfectly.
1-899-344-08-X £6.99

Funny Talk
edited by Jim Driver
A unique, informative and hilarious collection of new writing on – and around – the theme of comedy. Among the 25 authors: **Michael Palin** on Sid, the Python's driver, **Jeremy Hardy, Mark Lamarr, Max Bygraves** on his first car, **Mark Steel, Hattie Hayridge, Malcolm Hardee, Norman Lovett, Jon Ronson, Bob Mills**, plus all you ever need to know about good and terrible sit-coms, and 12 new cartoons from **Ray Lowry**. "Thoroughly excellent! " – *Time Out*
ISBN 1 899344 01 2 — £6.95

Deep & Meaningless
The complete JOHN OTWAY lyrics, compiled by John Haxby
The only complete collection of lyrics from the much-loved rock humorist, songwriter and best-selling author. Includes the hits *Really Free* and *Beware of the Flowers*, as well as rare pictures and sleeve shots.
1-899-344-07-1 £5.99

Passport to the Pub
The Tourist's Guide to Pub Etiquette by Kate Fox
(in association with the Brewers & Licensed Retailers Society)
Basic advice and information tourists (and others!) need in order to unravel the mysteries of Britain's pubs. Includes basic rules, do's and don'ts, warnings and tips. Very funny and surprisingly useful for anyone who ever has need to enter a British pub.
1-899-344-09-8 £3.99

All books published by The Do-Not Press are available at local bookshops or by post (post-free in UK, Ireland and other EC countries) from:

The Do-Not Press
PO Box 4215
London
SE23 2QD

Please allow twenty days for delivery and make cheques payable to:
"The Do-Not Press"

The Do-Not Press
Fiercely Independent Publishing

Keep in touch with what's happening at the cutting edge of independent British publishing.

Join The Do-Not Press Information Service and receive advance information of all our new titles, as well as news of events and launches in your area, and the occasional free gift and special offer.

Simply send your name and address to:
The Do-Not Press (Dept. ST)
PO Box 4215
London
SE23 2QD

There is no obligation to purchase and no salesman will call.